There was no future, Caroline knew, in her love for Andrew, who was married to a wife who loved and needed him. So she sought escape in far-off Mexico—where she fell in love with a man who was forbidden to her in a way Andrew had never been ...

Books you will enjoy
by ANNE MATHER

A HAUNTING COMPULSION

The affair between Rachel Williams and Jaime Shard had been over for years—but despite the bitterness she felt about Jaime, Rachel was still fond of his parents, and when they invited her to spend Christmas with them she could hardly refuse. But she had not realised that Jaime would be there too . . .

IMAGES OF LOVE

It was sheer coincidence that Mark Newman should turn out to be the half-brother of Robert Lang, who had ruined Tobie's life—but when Mark invited her to go with him to the Caribbean to meet his family, she could not resist the chance to see Robert again—and pay him back for what he had done to her. But Tobie didn't know what had happened to Robert since they had last met . . .

WHISPER OF DARKNESS

Why was Jake Sheldon so antagonistic to Joanna when he so desperately needed her as a governess for his difficult little daughter? Why did he persist in cutting both himself and the child off from all social contacts? Joanna asked herself the questions—but she should have been asking another one: Why was she so concerned about Jake?

THE INNOCENT INVADER

Sarah, straight from a convent, went out wide-eyed with excitement to the West Indies to a job as governess to the small ward of Jason de Cordova. And had the bad luck to fall in love with her employer—who was not only married but had every intention of staying married! How could she cope with the heartbreak?

FORBIDDEN FLAME

BY

ANNE MATHER

MILLS & BOON LIMITED
15–16 BROOK'S MEWS
LONDON W1A 1DR

First published 1981
Australian copyright 1981
Philippine copyright 1981
This edition 1981

© Anne Mather 1981

ISBN 0 263 73514 1

Set in 10 on 11 pt. Monophoto Baskerville

Made and printed in Great Britain by
Richard Clay (The Chaucer Press) Ltd,
Bungay, Suffolk

CHAPTER ONE

PEERING through the fly-spotted window of the hotel in Las Estadas, Caroline thought she must have been slightly mad to agree to come here. Whatever had possessed her to apply for this job? Why on earth had she imagined it would be exciting, a challenge, something to divert her from the sudden emptiness of her life in England? What did she, a university graduate, with honours in English and history, know of teaching an eight-year-old child, and why had she been chosen when there had obviously been others more suitable?

Of course, the advertisement she had read would have interested anyone with a spark of adventure in their blood. The chance to work in Mexico—the land of the Aztecs, steeped in history, and peopled by the ancestors of Montezuma and Cortez—but Caroline wondered now how many of those other applicants had baulked when they were expected to travel to a remote village north of Yucatan. She had spoken with several of the other girls, waiting in the drawing room of the hotel suite in London, and almost all of them had gained the opinion that they were to work in Mexico City.

But even when Caroline had learned where the job was she had not been discouraged. She knew a little about Mexico, or so she had imagined, and the idea of living within driving distance of the Mayan city of Chichen Itza had been a glowing inducement. Only now, waiting in the seedy surroundings of the Hotel Hermosa, a misnomer surely, did the full realisation of what she was committed to occur to her, and if there had been some way she could return to Merida without anyone's knowledge, she would have surely done so.

Outside, a drenching downpour had turned the street into a muddy river, and given a grey aspect to buildings already dirt-daubed and ramshackle. This was not the Mexico she had imagined, the colourful blending of past and present in a kaleidoscope of rich mosaics and even richer architecture. This was poverty and squalor, and the simple struggle for survival against enormous odds. Las Estadas had not yet felt the impact of the oil boom that was supposedly going to transform Mexico's economy. Here life was still held cheaply and governed by the whims of weather, and a seemingly unkind fate. To Caroline, used to the social and cultural advantages of a Western civilisation, the sight of so much deprivation was doubly shocking, and she was uncomfortably aware that she would have much preferred not to have seen what she had.

Turning away from the window, she viewed the sordid little room behind her without liking. A rag mat beside the narrow iron-railed bedspread was all the covering the floor possessed, and the water in the chipped jug on the washstand was the graveyard for the assortment of insects who had drowned there during the night. The bed itself had been lumpy and not particularly clean, but the night before Caroline had been so tired she felt she could have slept on the floor. This morning, however, she had experienced a shudder of revulsion when she saw the grubby sheets in daylight, and the breakfast of hot *tortillas* and strong-smelling coffee still stood on the rickety table where the obsequious hotel proprietor had left it.

A knock at her door brought an automatic stiffening of her spine, and she straightened away from the window to stand rather apprehensively in the middle of the floor. 'Who is it?' she called, clasping her slim fingers tightly together, and then mentally sagged again when Señor Allende put his head round the door.

'*El desayuno, señorita*—it was okay?'

The hotel proprietor was enormously fat, and as he eased his way into the room, Caroline couldn't help wondering how many of those people she had seen could have lived on what he ate. His girth was disgusting, and he brought with him an odour of sweat and sour *tequila* that caused her empty stomach to heave.

'Ah—but you have not eaten!' he exclaimed now, observing the untouched tray. 'It is not to your liking, *señorita*? You want I should have Maria make you something else?'

'Thank you, no.' Caroline shook her head firmly. 'I—er—I'm not hungry. Could you tell me again, what time did Señor Montejo say he would be here?'

'Don Esteban say he will come before noon,' responded the fat little Mexican thoughtfully, stroking his black moustaches, and viewing Caroline's slim figure with an irritatingly speculative eye. '*Mas, por cierto, el tiempo*—the weather, you understand? It may cause—how you say—the delay, *no*?'

Caroline's spirits sank even further. 'You mean the roads may be impassable?' she suggested, and Señor Allende nodded.

'Is possible,' he agreed. Then he smiled, revealing tobacco-stained teeth. '*Mas*, no worry, *señorita*. Jose,' he pointed to himself, 'Jose take good care of you, till Don Esteban come.'

'Yes.'

Caroline forced a faint smile of acknowledgement, but she was not enthusiastic. She would not welcome having to spend another night between those dubious sheets, and Señor Allende's attitude grew increasingly proprietorial. He was looking at her now, as if he had some prior claim to her loyalties, while she felt she would have preferred any other hotel to this. But Señor Montejo had made the arrangements, and she could only assume that this was the best Las Estadas had to offer.

'So——' Señor Allende drew a fat cigar out of his waistcoat pocket, bit off the end and spat it repulsively on to the floor. 'Why do you not come downstairs and wait in my office, *no*? I have a little bottle of something there to—how do you say it?—make the day sunny, hm?'

He pronounced little as 'leetle', and it was all Caroline could do not to grimace outright. Did he really imagine she might find his company appealing? If she had not felt so absurdly vulnerable, she could have laughed at the predictability of it all. As it was, she took a backward step and shook her head politely but firmly.

'I don't think so, thank you,' she replied crisply. 'I'll stay here. I can watch the street from my window, and I wouldn't want to put you to any trouble.'

'Is no trouble,' exclaimed Señor Allende, spreading his hands in typically Latin fashion. 'Come——' He stretched out one podgy hand. 'Is much nicer downstairs.'

'No!' Caroline was very definite this time. 'Please—I prefer to be alone. If you'll excuse me——'

Señor Allende shrugged, and then his small eyes narrowed between the folds of flesh. 'Okay, okay, is no big deal,' he retorted. '*Como quiere usted!*' And with another shrug of his shoulders, he left her, closing the door behind him with heavy definition.

Caroline ran a relieved hand over the crown of her head and down to her nape, resting her head back against the support, expelling the tension that had briefly gripped her. The last thing she needed was complications of that sort, and she let her shoulders droop as she walked wearily back to the window. Where was Señor Montejo? Surely a night's rain was not sufficient to cut all communications!

Pressing her palms together, she put her thumbs against her lips and gazed thoughtfully down at the verandah opposite. For the first time she questioned her own expectations of her destination. What would the Montejo house be like? What would Señor Montejo be like? And how could she have been foolish enough to commit herself to a whole month's probation, when she might conceivably want to leave after only one day?

Somehow things had seemed so different in London. No one meeting Señora Garcia, who had conducted the interviews, could have had any doubts that anyone associated with her—and she was the child's grandmother—could live in anything other than exemplary surroundings. She had exuded an aura of wealth and sophistication, in keeping with the Dior suit and Cartier pearls she was wearing, and Caroline had naturally assumed her son-in-law and his daughter would be the same. Perhaps she was wrong. Perhaps Señora Garcia's daughter had married beneath her. Perhaps Señor Montejo would turn out to be more like Señor Allende . . .

At noon, the buxom cook, Maria, brought her a bowl of greasy stew and some corn bread. Caroline suffered herself to eat a little of the stew and all of the bread, realising it would be foolish to starve herself in this climate, and then returned to her seat by the window, wondering idly if the road to Merida was still open.

The afternoon dragged on, and Caroline grew increasingly anxious. What if, as seemed likely, Señor Montejo did not come? How many days might she be expected to stay in this awful place?

Her eyes wandered restlessly up and down the street, watching the struggle an ancient truck was having trying to gain purchase on the slippery road, silently sympathising as its churning wheels threw a shower of mud over an elderly woman passing by. An ox-cart made better progress, though the rain was no less heavy, and she turned away, sighing, just as the door to her room burst open.

It was late afternoon, and the low-hanging clouds had

left the room in partial shadow, but the hotel proprietor's bulk was unmistakable. He stood swaying on the threshold, an opened bottle of *tequila* clutched in his hand, and Caroline had no need to wonder how he had spent the day.

'*Holà, señorita!*' he greeted her unsteadily, raising the bottle to his mouth and taking a greedy draught. 'Perhaps you like Jose's com-company now, hm? You share a little drink with Jose, *si*?'

Caroline knew she mustn't panic. She was not exactly afraid, but she was alarmed, and although she felt reasonably capable of defending herself, should the need arise, she dreaded to think where she might go if he threw her out.

'I don't drink, Señor Allende,' she said now, facing him bravely. At five feet six inches, she was almost half a head taller than he was, and infinitely fitter, if his size was anything to go by.

'Do-don't drink!' he echoed, stumbling a little over his words. '*Por cierto*, you take a little *tequila*. *Tequila* is good, very good. You try some—here—here——'

He came towards her heavily, holding out the bottle, urging her to take a mouthful. Caroline's stomach lurched as she stepped aside. The idea of putting her lips where his greasy mouth had been caused the lumpy stew to rise into the back of her throat like bile, and she swallowed it back nauseously, shifting to avoid his reaching fingers.

'Señor Allende, please! I don't want to try any,' she protested, moving round the bed, but he only came after her, like some lumbering buffalo, panting as his thoughts accelerated beyond the pursuit.

'You try, you try,' he said, over and over again, licking his lips in anticipation, and Caroline realised it was going to be impossible to get out of this without a struggle.

She was backed into a corner of the room, with the bed

on one side, and the wall of the room, with its tiny crucifix, on the other, and her eyes turned despairingly from
the religious image. No immortal being could help her
now, and with sudden inspiration she sprang on to the
bed, blessing her corded jeans that provided no swirling
skirts for the man to grasp. But the proprietor was more
agile than she thought, or perhaps desperation lent him
speed. Whatever the truth of the matter, his plump
fingers reached surely for her ankle, and his brutal jerk
brought her down on the bed, the unyielding mattress
almost knocking the breath from her body. In those first
stunned moments, she felt him clambering on to the bed
beside her, and now she really did panic. With a strength
she hardly knew she possessed, she twisted on to her back,
drawing up her knee in one swift motion, bringing it to
the fleshy underside of his body with purposeful effect.
His agonised groan was audible, and she scrambled out
from beneath him, reaching the door just as another man
was about to enter. She collided helplessly with his hard
body, and he had to grasp her shoulders to save himself.
In the grip of panic, Caroline had no thought to his identity, imagining this might be some colleague of Señor
Allende come to join the fun, but as she lifted her foot to
deliver a similar blow, he swung her about, imprisoning
her arms by her side.

'*Basta, basta!*' he exclaimed, half angrily, then lifted his
eyes to the figure just endeavouring to climb off the bed.
With Caroline still struggling in his arms, he stared
grimly at the obese hotel proprietor, and then, speaking
in English for her benefit, he said: 'What has been going
on here, Allende? Did you get a little more than you had
expected?'

The cultured voice, accented though it was, brought
Caroline to her senses. His words, and the contemptuous
way he said them, made her instantly aware that this was
no coarse drinking partner of the sweating little pro-

prietor. Even without Señor Allende's air of subdued discomfort, she would have known that this was someone to
be reckoned with, and her struggles stilled as he politely
released her.

'I—I'm sorry if I hurt you——' she began, turning
with some gratitude to her rescuer, then her speech died
away beneath the hooded grey eyes of the man confront-
ing her.

Señor Montejo, if it was indeed he, was like nothing
she had imagined. He was younger, for one thing, certainly no more than thirty, and taller than most of the
men she had seen since she arrived in Mexico. He was
very dark, dark-haired and olive-skinned, but his features
possessed all the unconscious hauteur of his Spanish fore-
bears. He was not handsome in the accepted sense of the
word. His brows were too strongly marked, his cheek-
bones too hard, his mouth too thin—but he was devastat-
ingly attractive, and the dark linen jacket and pants he
was wearing, over a darker brown fine wool shirt, hugged
his wide shoulders and muscular thighs like a second skin.
Caroline had never met anyone who exuded such an aura
of raw masculinity, and for a moment she faltered, at
once confused and embarrassed.

'Señor, señor—' Taking advantage of Caroline's discomfort, the hotel proprietor was attempting to defend
himself. 'You misunderstand, señor——'

'I think not.' Señor Montejo's voice was deep and attractive. 'I find you, Allende, in a position of some—shall
we say, discomfort, on Señorita Leyton's bed, and the
señorita herself evidently in some distress——'

'Unnecessarily, I assure you, señor!' protested Señor
Allende dramatically. 'I have—I admit it—had a little
too much to drink.' He shrugged expressively. 'So I rest
for un momento on the señorita's bed. Que he hecho?'

'What were you doing in the señorita's room?' enquired
Montejo pleasantly, but Caroline could hear the underly-

ing core of steel in his voice.

'Perhaps—it was a misunderstanding,' she murmured unhappily, unwilling to make enemies within twenty-four hours of her arrival. 'I—I don't think Señor Allende meant any harm——'

Montejo's dark face assumed an ironic expression. 'Do you not?' He tilted his head in Allende's direction. 'You are fortunate that Miss Leyton is not vindictive, my friend. I do not think my brother would be so generous.'

Señor Allende spread his hands. 'You will not tell Don Esteban, *señor*. This *posada* is all I have——'

The man made an indifferent gesture and said something else in their own language, but Caroline was not paying any attention. Something else, something Señor Allende had said, caused her to revise her first opinion, and she realised with sudden perception that this man was not her employer. Yet he knew her name, and he had mentioned his brother. But who was he? Señora Garcia had mentioned no brother. Only that her son-in-law was a widower, living alone with his daughter and an elderly aunt, on the family's estates at San Luis de Merced.

As if becoming aware of her doubts and confusion, the man turned back to her now, performing a slight bow, and saying politely: 'Forgive me, Miss Leyton. I have not introduced myself. My name is Montejo, Luis Vincente de Montejo, brother to Don Esteban, and uncle to your charge, Doña Emilia.'

'I see.' Caroline gathered herself quickly. 'You are—you are here to meet me?'

'Of course.' Long dark lashes narrowed the steel grey eyes. 'My brother is—indisposed. He asked me to bring you to San Luis.'

Caroline drew a somewhat unsteady breath and nodded. 'I'll get my things.'

'Permit me.'

He was there before her, hefting her two cases effortlessly, indicating that she should preceded him from the room. The fat little hotel proprietor watched them with a mixture of relief and brooding resentment, and Caroline, meeting his cold gaze, shivered. In spite of the ingratiating smile he immediately adopted, she would not trust him an inch, and she hoped she never had to throw herself on his mercy.

Downstairs, a group of men were gathered in the hall, and from their attitude Caroline suspected they had been hoping for a fight. She guessed they had known what Allende was about, and as they stepped back with evident respect to let them pass, she felt an increasing surge of gratitude towards Señor Montejo. Without his intervention she could have expected no help from this quarter, and she pressed her arms tightly against her sides to avoid any kind of contact.

Outside, the downpour had eased somewhat, but it was still raining. Water drained in douches from the eaves above their heads as they crossed the muddy street to where a scarcely-identifiable Range Rover was parked, and the shoulders of Caroline's shirt felt damp as she scrambled with more haste than elegance into the front seat. Her companion thrust her cases into the back, then came round the bonnet to get in beside her, removing his jacket as he did so, and tossing it into the back along with her luggage.

He didn't say anything as he inserted the keys into the ignition and started the engine, and Caroline endeavoured to recover her composure. It wasn't easy, with the memory of what had almost happened still sharply etched in her mind, but as her breathing slowed she managed to get it into some kind of perspective. In retrospect, it seemed almost ludicrous to imagine herself tumbling across the bed, but at the time she had known definite fear.

'A baptism of fire, would you say?' Señor Montejo enquired, as the vehicle reached the end of the village street, and Caroline glanced sideways at him. Ahead was only jungle, vine-infested and menacing in the fading grey light, and although Las Estadas was scarcely civilised, compared to what was beyond, the lights of the village seemed infinitely comforting. What more did she know of this man, after all? she pondered. Only what he had told her. And Señor Allende's behaviour, which had spoken of fear, as well as respect. But fear of what, and of whom, she had yet to find out.

'How—how far is it to San Luis de Merced?' she ventured, not answering him, and his mouth drew down at the corners.

'Not far,' he replied evenly. 'Between twenty and twenty-five miles. Why?' He was perceptive. 'Are you afraid you cannot trust me either?'

Caroline moistened her lips. 'Can I?'

He inclined his head. 'Of a surety, *señorita*.' He paused. 'Believe me, you have nothing to fear from me.'

It was dark long before they reached their destination. It came quickly, shrouding the surrounding trees in a cloak of shadows, hiding the primitive landscape, concealing the sparse settlements, much like Las Estadas, if not in size, then certainly in appearance. Caroline wondered how these people lived in such conditions, where they worked, how they supported themselves, what kind of education their children had. There seemed such a gulf between the man beside her and these poor peasants, but she was loath to voice it when he did not.

The road did improve for some distance, when they joined an interstate highway; but after a while they left it again to bounce heavily along a rutted track, liberally spread with potholes. Caroline gripped her seat very tightly, to prevent herself from being thrown against the man beside her, and she felt, rather than saw, him look her way.

'Are you regretting coming, *señorita*?' he asked, again surprising her by his perception. 'Do not be discouraged by the weather. It is not always like this. Tomorrow, the sun will shine, and you will see beauty as well as ugliness.'

Caroline turned her head. 'You admit—there is ugliness?'

'There is ugliness everywhere, *señorita*,' he replied flatly. 'All I am saying is, do not judge my country by its weaknesses. If you look for strength, you will find it.'

Caroline hesitated. 'That's a very profound view.'

'Profundity is as easy for a stupid man to mouth as a learned one,' he remarked, and she saw him smile in the illumination from the dials in front of him. 'Do not be misled by my enthusiasm. I love my country, that is all.'

Caroline was intrigued, as much by the man as by what he had said. He was a very attractive man, but she had known that as soon as she saw him. What she had not known then was that he had a sense of humour, or that she should find his conversation so stimulating.

'Your brother,' she said thoughtfully, 'he runs a ranch, doesn't he? Do you work with him?'

There was a moment's silence before he answered her, and then he said: 'Here, we call it a *hacienda*. And yes, Esteban is the *hacendado*. But he does not run the ranch. He has a—how do you call it?—overseer to run the spread for him.'

'And what do you grow? Corn? Maize?'

'Cattle,' responded Luis Montejo dryly. 'My brother employs many *gauchos*. It is a very large holding.'

Caroline nodded. She had known this. Señora Garcia had told her. And about her granddaughter, Emilia ...

'Your niece,' she tendered now. 'She's an only child, I believe.'

Again there was a pause before he replied. 'Yes,' he said at last. 'Emilia has no brothers or sisters. Her mother died when she was born.'

'Oh!' Señora Garcia had not told her this. 'How distressing for your brother! He must have been very upset.'

'Yes.'

It was an acknowledgement, no more, and Caroline found herself wondering whether she was mistaken in thinking his tone was clipped. Surely there was no suggestion that Don Esteban was uncaring of his wife's death. Surely Señora Garcia would have warned her if this was so.

Yet, she realised, she really knew nothing of these people, beyond what they chose to tell her. That was why her own parents had been so opposed to her travelling so far on such a slender recommendation. If they had not felt equally strongly about her relationship with Andrew Lovell, she knew they would have done their utmost to make her change her mind. As it was, they were torn in conflicting directions.

'So, you are young to have come so far alone,' Luis Montejo remarked, unconsciously interpreting her silence. 'But then,' he continued, an ironic twist to his lips, 'English girls are more emancipated than Spanish women. They do not have the restrictions put upon them as our girls do.'

Caroline struggled to recover her earlier enthusiasm. 'Do you disapprove, *señor*?' she ventured, forcing a light tone, and waited with some misgivings for his answer.

'It is not my concern,' he responded, moving his shoulders in a gesture of dismissal, and Caroline knew a moment's impatience.

'You must have an opinion,' she insisted, curious to know his feelings, and with a rueful grimace he avoided a pothole before replying.

'Let us say I have the usual chauvinist attitudes,' he remarked. 'A woman is not a man, and she should not try to emulate one.'

'You think that's what I'm trying to do?' exclaimed Caroline indignantly, and his laughter was low and attractive.

'No one could mistake your sex, *señorita*,' he assured her dryly, and she felt a not unpleasant stirring of her senses. 'All I am saying is that a woman's role is not naturally that of the hunter, but that the inevitable conclusion to any continued adaptation is transformation.'

Caroline gazed ahead of her, watching the headlights of the Range Rover as they searched out a marsh cactus, glimpsing, as if in a shadowy reflection, a four-legged creature moving out there in the darkness. His answer had been predictable, and yet more logical, than some she had heard. But it was not flattering to find oneself compared, however indirectly, to a member of the opposite sex, and she wished she had some clever response to flatten his biased argument.

'I have offended you, I think,' he commented now, his tone lacking its earlier mockery. 'I am sorry, I did not mean to do so. But you asked for my opinion, and I gave it.'

Caroline shrugged. 'You haven't offended me,' she declared, although, unknowingly, her whole demeanour suggested that he had. 'I was trying to think of a suitable answer, that's all.'

'I think you mean a suitable set-down,' he observed, giving her a wry grin. 'I am sorry, truly. Believe me, you are a very feminine lady, and I salute your courage in pursuing your career.'

'You don't really.' Caroline would not be deceived. 'You're probably one of those men who thinks a woman shouldn't have a brain in her head!'

'No!' His humour was infectious, and against her will Caroline found herself responding to it.

'You do,' she insisted, abandoning all formality between them. 'I just hope your brother is more tolerant in his attitudes to women.'

There was another of those pregnant silences, when Caroline wondered exactly what she had said, and when he replied, there was little humour left in his voice. 'Oh, yes,' he said, and she heard the irony in his tones, 'Esteban is much more tolerant you will find. It was he who employed you, *señorita*. How could he think otherwise?'

It was not the answer she would have preferred, and she was left feeling decidedly deflated. For a few minutes she had lost the feeling of apprehension that had gripped her ever since Señor Allende burst into her room. But once again a sense of unease enveloped her, making her overwhelmingly aware of her own vulnerability.

'How—how much further is it?' she asked now, needing his voice to dispel her tension, and he frowned into the darkness.

'Not far,' he told her. 'Five miles, at most. Are you tired? Or perhaps hungry? I am sure my brother's housekeeper will have a meal waiting for you.'

'And—and your aunt?' Caroline probed. 'Señora Garcia told me she also lives at the—the *hacienda*.'

'That is correct. She came to San Luis when my father married her sister. She has never married, and she considers San Luis her home.'

Caroline welcomed this information. An elderly aunt sounded infinitely less intimidating than a man whose wife had died in childbirth, and who might or might not have mourned her passing. She stared out blindly into the darkness. It seemed such a long way. The road was so bad, and so twisting. Was this the only link with civilisation?

She was not thinking what she was doing, slumped in her seat, wrapped in the corkscrewing spiral of her thoughts. When the Range Rover swung round a bend in the road, and Señor Montejo braked hard to avoid a pile of rocks and debris brought down by the rain, she was flung about like a doll, cracking her head on the wind-screen before being thrown back against him. It happened so suddenly she was unable to save herself, and she clutched at him violently, to prevent further punishment.

'*Dios mío!*' he muttered, as the vehicle shuddered to a standstill, and his arm automatically went around her. 'Are you all right? Did I hurt you? I am sorry. This road can be treacherous after a storm.'

Caroline breathed shakily, her face pressed against the soft material of his shirt. Beneath the fine cloth, his heart was pounding heavily in her ears, and the clean male scent of his skin filled her nostrils. His body was hard, muscular, unyielding, and yet possessed of a supple strength, that accommodated the flexibility of hers. Even after the Range Rover had ground to a halt, and the uncanny silence had enveloped them in its blanketing shield, she clung to his strength, and knew it was not just the near-accident which had aroused such a desire for his protection.

'Miss Leyton!' His voice was a key lower, husky, possessed of a certain restraint. 'Miss Leyton, what is it? Are you hurt? Tell me, what is the matter?'

His words brought Caroline to her senses, and with a little gesture of negation she moved away from him. Immediately he withdrew his arm from the back of her seat, and after allowing her a swift appraisal, he thrust open his door.

Sliding his arms into his jacket, he retrieved a spade from the back of the vehicle, and while she endeavoured to compose herself, he vigorously disposed of the pile of debris. He worked in the illumination from the head-lights, bending and lifting, and throwing the contents of the spade across the ditch at the side of the road. Caroline watched him with uneasy awareness, troubled as much by her own reactions to him as by their brush with danger. It was disturbing to realise that during those moments in his arms she had known a wholly unexpected sense of anticipation, and she knew if he had chosen to bend his head and find her mouth with his she would not have objected.

It was a shocking realisation, not only because of her feelings for Andrew, but because she had known Luis Montejo for such a short period of time. She had thought herself so self-confident, so emancipated—yet, when the warm scent of his breath had brushed her cheek, she had felt as weak and susceptible as any Victorian miss. She checked the shoulder-length curve of her hair with unsteady fingers. No doubt he had known how she felt, she thought, with some self-derision. He must be highly amused now, after her previous assertions of female rights. Perhaps she should be grateful he had not chosen to take the affair any further. It would have been doubly humiliating to arrive on Don Esteban's doorstep, with his brother's brand already upon her.

The spade thudded into the back of the vehicle, and she stiffened as the door beside her opened, and Luis Montejo climbed back into his seat. This time, he kept his jacket on, and the damp smell of the material mingled with the faint odour of sweat from his exertions.

'You are sure you are all right?' he enquired again, his voice perceptibly cooler now, yet still polite and concerned, and she nodded, fingering a slight swelling on her temple.

'I should have been more careful,' she answered, endeavouring to keep her tone light. 'Your roads are certainly—unpredictable.'

'And dangerous,' he agreed, with grim impatience, starting the engine abruptly and thrusting it into drive, and Caroline turned her head away from him, to gaze through the rain-smeared window.

San Luis de Merced was a village, as well as the place where Don Esteban de Montejo had his estates. There were lights in the village, glowing through the shutters of adobe dwellings, mingling with the smoke from a dozen chimneys. There was the spicy smell of meat and peppers, and the stronger aroma of woodsmoke, and children in open doorways, to watch their progress. Someone shouted after them, and Luis Montejo answered, raising his hand in greeting as Caroline thought she heard the word 'padre'. But her attention was diverted as the Range Rover lurched on to an upward slope, and she clung desperately to her seat as they wound precipitously up through a belt of trees, to where high wooden gates were set in a grey stone wall. The wall itself was easily eight feet high, a solid barrier to what was beyond, and Caroline's nerves tightened. Beyond the wall was her destination, and her courage faltered at the sight of that prison-like edifice.

Luis Montejo brought the vehicle to a halt and sprang down again to hammer on the gates. Reassuringly, they were soon opened, by an elderly retainer, dressed in the usual garb of loose-fitting pants, and waistcoat, the sleeves of his shirt rolled back to his elbows. He removed the wide-brimmed hat from his head as they drove through, then replaced it again to close the gates behind them.

'Gomez,' remarked her companion shortly, as Caroline glanced back over her shoulder. 'He used to work for my brother, but now he is too old to ride herd, and spends his days keeping the gate.'

'Like St Peter,' commented Caroline, wishing to ease the tension inside her, and Luis Montejo gave her a thoughtful look.

'Perhaps,' he conceded at length, but Caroline had the distinct impression that he had been tempted to make another comparison.

Beyond the gates, the tyres encountered the solid mass of a stone courtyard. Caroline decided it resembled an ancient fortress, with its outer walls and solid buttresses, a width of drive leading past stables and outhouses and under an inner archway to the stone-flagged entrance.

Montejo drove under the arch, and brought the Range Rover to a halt at the foot of a flight of steps, leading up to a wooden door. The rain had ceased, and the warmth of the night air dispelled the feeling of chill Caroline had developed when first she saw the house. There was the fragrant scent of oleander and hibiscus, and the soft smell of earth after rain, and as she climbed out of the vehicle Caroline determined not to allow what had happened in Las Estadas to influence her first impressions of her home for the next few weeks.

The door above them opened as Luis Montejo was unloading her cases from the Range Rover. A plump, round-faced little woman descended the steps to greet them, and meeting her round, beady little eyes, Caroline wondered if this could conceivably be Doña Isabel. She was quickly disillusioned.

'Consuelo,' remarked the man beside her, straightening with a case in each hand. 'She speaks little English, but she will do her best.'

'*Buenas tardes, señor.*' Consuelo addressed herself to Luis Montejo, but her eyes were all for Caroline. '*Buenas tardes, señorita. Bienvenido a San Luis.*'

'Thank you—*gracias!*' It was one of the few words she knew and Caroline glanced in some embarrassment towards Señor Montejo, doubting the accuracy of her accent.

But he merely inclined his head and said '*Muy bien,*' in a low voice behind her, as they followed the gesticulating Consuelo up the steps. '*No sabia que pedia hablar español!*' he added, confusing her further, and she glanced round at him, pursing her lips.

'You must know I don't understand you,' she whispered, aware of Consuelo's inquisitive interest, and his smile was a disturbing reminder of the way he had made her feel in the car.

'*No importa*,' he assured her, his meaning obvious this time, and she sighed. 'Esteban was educated at Oxford. I am sure you will have no difficulty in understanding him.'

The undertones of his words were lost on her as she stepped into the baroque beauty of the exquisitely decorated hall of the house. In the light from a dozen electric lamps, concealed behind bronze shades, her eyes were dazzled by fluted columns supporting the high arched ceiling, by heavily carved mouldings and inlaid mosaics, and by miniaturised statues of the Virgin and Child. The vertiginous twists of a wrought-iron staircase were enhanced by leaves veined in marble, and the chequerboard pattern beneath their feet was coloured in black and gold. If the outer appearance of the house had been daunting, its inner beauty more than made up for it, and she turned to the man behind her with bewildered eyes, seeking some explanation.

'As you can see, my brother lives in style, *señorita*,' Luis Montejo remarked mockingly, and before she could make any protest at his own apparent acceptance of the situation, another voice broke in on them.

'Señorita Leyton!' it enquired, in vaguely slurred tones. 'It is Señorita Leyton, is it not? *Ola*, welcome to the Hacienda Montejo, *señorita*. I hope you are going to be very happy here.'

Caroline turned half guiltily, aware of the disloyalty of her thoughts only moments before, to find a man approaching them across the expanse of black and gold marble. If this was Esteban Montejo, and she had every reason to suppose it was, he, too, was tall, though not so tall as his brother, and of much heavier build. Like his surroundings, he looked immaculate, in a formal evening suit of seamed black pants and white jacket, his only apparent concession to the heat, the printed silk cravat about his throat, instead of the usual white tie. But what disturbed Caroline most was the unevenness of his approach; the way he placed each foot with evident precision, and the faintly smug expression he adopted as he neared her.

'My brother, Don Esteban,' observed Luis Montejo, with studied politeness, and Caroline felt her hand captured and raised almost to Don Esteban's lips.

'I am most happy to meet you, *señorita*,' Don Esteban assured her ardently, and the odour on his breath was unmistakable. Was this the indisposition his brother had hinted at? Caroline wondered faintly, smothering her revulsion, and knew a moment's incredulity that features that had so much in common should be so amazingly different.

Realising she had to say something to retrieve her hand, she forced a smile. 'You—you have a beautiful home, *señor*,' she said, determinedly withdrawing her fingers from his. 'It—well, it's not at all what I expected.'

Don Esteban rocked back on his heels, casting a satisfied glance towards the intricately-carved ceiling, the white walls and pilasters, the iron balustrade that formed a gallery above them. 'You like it?' he drawled. 'It is a modest dwelling compared to the palaces my family left behind them in Cadiz, *señorita*.' He shrugged. 'But——' and here his dark eyes, much darker than those of his brother, returned to her face, 'it serves the purpose. And there is room enough for the three members of my family who live here.'

'Oh, but——' Caroline's brows ascended, and she glanced in some confusion towards the man who had brought her here. How could there only be *three* members?

And as if understanding that silent enquiry, Don Esteban spoke again. 'My brother?' he suggested. 'Luis?' His tongue slurred over the man's name. 'Did he not tell you, *señorita*? Did he not explain?' His lips curled. 'My brother does not live with us here at San Luis, Miss Leyton. Like his namesake, Luis is in search of immortality also. He lives in Mariposa, *señorita*. At the seminary of San Pedro de Alcantara.'

CHAPTER TWO

CAROLINE awakened with the instinctive awareness that all was not well. For a few minutes she lay still in the middle of the huge baroque bed, with its carved head-board and gilded hangings, once used, Don Esteban had assured her, by the Emperor Maximilian himself, and let the events of the previous evening sweep over her in inti-mate detail. And then, loath to spoil the new day with such reminiscences, she thrust back the silken coverings and put her feet to the floor.

There was a rug beside her bed, a soft silky alpaca rug, into which her toes curled, and she allowed its sensuous touch to soothe her unquiet thoughts. No matter what she had let herself into here, she was committed to stay for at least four weeks, she told herself severely, but it was not an easy fact to accept.

The night before had been like something out of a dream, or perhaps a nightmare described it more aptly. Remembering the dinner she had shared with the two brothers, she shuddered in revulsion, and her palms found her cheeks as she recalled that grotesque meal in its en-tirety.

It had been obvious from the start that Don Esteban was by no means sober, and the amount of wine served with the meal had only exaggerated his condition. They had eaten in the ornate dining room, at a table large enough to seat a score of guests, and from silver and crystal worth a small fortune. They were served by an army of waiters, and offered a fantastic number of courses, each cooked and presented with a different sauce. There were several courses of fish, from a spicy stuffed variety to the lightest of shellfish mousses, chilled soups, steaming consommés, wine-flavoured and aromatic, chicken served in wine and cream, stuffed *tamales, enchiladas,* deliciously filled with cheese, pork served with apples and tomatoes and onions, and every kind of fruit imaginable.

Caroline had eaten little, aware of the dangers of too much rich food on a stomach already churning with nerves, and she had noticed Don Esteban followed her example. But he had continually filled his glass, watching her intently across the expanse of polished mahogany, probing and assessing, and making her overwhelmingly aware that he found her presence at his table pleasing to him.

Luis Montejo had eaten more enthusiastically, drinking only a little wine, keeping his thoughts to himself. It had been left to Caroline to answer Don Esteban's questions, and to listen in shocked fascination as he deliberately proceeded to provoke his brother.

Remembering it all now, Caroline rose from the bed and padded barefoot across to the window. Without the benefit of the rug, the tiled floor was cool to her feet, but she scarcely noticed. Drawing the heavy curtains aside, she opened the window, and gasped with sudden wonder at the beauty of the view.

Last night there had been nothing to be seen, only darkness, and the troubling obscurity of her own thoughts. But this morning the sun was shining, and even the enclosing wall that surrounded the property had taken on a rose-coloured hue.

But it was beyond the wall that Caroline's eyes were drawn, to the flower-strewn banks of a river flowing through rugged but open land to where a church tower stood silhouetted against the sky. Her eyes followed the river as it rushed through a narrow gorge to disappear from sight, only to appear again in the shimmering distance, a spreading, shifting expanse of water. Caroline blinked. That was no river, she realised in sudden excitement. It was the sea. Only the sea could give that blue-green tinge to the horizon, and her spirits soared. She had known Yucatan was a peninsula but somehow she had never imagined San Luis de Merced might be near the sea. She gazed at it eagerly, savouring its familiarity, and breathing deeply, as if she could already taste its salty flavour.

With an effort she allowed her attention to be caught by a movement near at hand. There was a herd of cattle grazing some distance from the house, and her eyes widened at their number. There must be hundreds, she thought incredulously, then wondered with some misgivings if one had to negotiate the herds to reach the estuary.

She sighed. No doubt she would find out. But once again the more immediate present gripped her, reminding her that she had yet to meet her charge, the young Emilia, or the elderly retainer, Doña Isabel.

There was a bathroom adjoining the bedroom, and checking that it was still quite early, barely eight o'clock in fact, she went to take a shower. She had been too exhausted the night before to do anything more than wash her face and hands and clean her teeth, but now she surveyed the bathroom's luxurious appointments with more enthusiasm.

Like everything else, the bathroom was ornate. The walls were lined with gilded mirrors, the taps on the bath and handbasin were gold-plated, and even the shower had a gold-plated spray. Still, the water was hot, and refusing to allow the memory of how the majority of the population lived to deter her, Caroline pulled on a shower cap and stepped beneath the invigorating cascade.

Towelling herself dry, she returned to the bedroom again, viewing her still-packed cases with some distaste. They would have to wait until she discovered what her duties were going to be, she decided, and determinedly dismissed the fleeting urge to beg Luis to take her with him when he left for Mariposa.

Dropping the towel, she rummaged for clean underwear, but when she turned back, the shred of cream cotton clutched in her hand, she encountered her reflection in the long gilded cheval mirrors. They were very narcissistic mirrors, she realised, folding one upon the other, throwing back her image from every angle. But they were candid, too, in their search for perfection, and there was no way one could disguise any possible flaw.

Reluctantly, Caroline allowed herself a moment's assessment. Her body was slim, without being angular, her hips shaped, her legs long and attractive. She sometimes thought her legs were her best feature, although Andrew had insisted she had equally desirable attributes elsewhere. Her tongue circled lips that were unknowingly sensuous, troubled a little by her thoughts at that moment. It was not of Andrew that she was thinking but of Luis de Montejo, and her own disturbing awareness of him as a man. She had never met a man quite like him before, but then she had never had a conversation with a Roman Catholic priest before. Mr Thomas, the Church of England vicar at St David's back home, bore no resemblance to the man who had rescued her from Señor Allende's unwanted attentions, and even now she found it difficult to associate Luis with the Church.

Luis! The way his name came so easily to her tongue was disturbing, too, and she drew her lower lip between

her teeth, nibbling on it uneasily. Unwillingly she recalled Don Esteban's behaviour over dinner. His attitude
towards his brother had been deliberately offensive, and,
as the evening progressed, increasingly crude. He had
spoken of things in Caroline's presence, things which even
she, in her self-asserted role of emancipist, would have
preferred not to hear, and she had badly wanted to
escape. When he baited Luis, when he made a mockery
of his tolerance towards the people, when he spoke of his
celibacy, Caroline had wanted to die of embarrassment,
but Don Esteban had seemed to enjoy her discomfort far
more than his brother's indifference.

And Luis had maintained a façade of detachment,
whether it was real or otherwise. He had refused to
answer his brother's coarser comments, and adopted an
air of resigned fortitude, that succeeded inasmuch as it
seemed to drive Don Esteban almost to distraction. His
speech got more slurred, he filled his glass more frequently, and finally slumped in his chair, the victim of his
own frustration. Several of the servants came at once to
carry him to bed, almost as if this was a regular occurrence, and Caroline had been left to face Luis's intent
appraisal, with the distinct perception of her own inadequacy.

She had wanted to rant at him then, to accuse him of
knowing to what he was bringing her, to question his
integrity in allowing her to believe that his brother was
an ordinary man—but she hadn't. How could she blame
him for her own foolhardiness? How could she despise
him, when she had chosen this job? If anyone was to
blame, it was Señora Garcia, in deceiving her so completely; although even that imposition didn't hold water,
when she considered how ambiguously the advertisement
had been worded. It was her own fault, and hers alone.
She had accepted the post, she had come here with such a
high opinion of her own capabilities, and if it proved to

be a disaster then she would have to extricate herself.

She gave a grim little smile now, as she recalled their conversation on the way to San Luis de Merced. What must he have been thinking when she made her stand for women's liberation? How subtly he had avoided discussing his brother's position. He must have known how soon her eyes would be opened, and yet not then, or last evening, had he voiced the obvious cliché.

With an exclamation of impatience she put on her scanty underwear and reached for the simple pleated skirt, folded on top of her suitcase. The matching silk shirt that went with it was the colour of African violets, and the outfit was in sharp contrast to the pale fall of ash-blonde hair. Her hair was straight and silky, smooth from a centre parting, and ideal in this climate, where more elaborate styles would droop with the humidity. She could wash it and dry it in an hour, without requiring any artificial assistance.

She was smoothing a shiny lip-gloss on to her mouth when there was a knock at her door. Half turning, she called: 'Come in!' and after a few moments' pause the door was tentatively opened. A young Indian girl stood just outside, holding a tray. She was attired in the black dress and white apron, which seemed to be uniform for all the female staff, and she ducked her head politely, and said: '*Desayuno, por favor, señorita. Puedo entrar?*'

Caroline put down her lip brush and smiled. 'You can put the tray over there,' she said, indicating the marble-topped table near the windows, and then, summoning what little of the language she could remember, she added: '*Su nombre—que es?*'

The girl put down the tray and straightened nervously, folding her hands together. 'Carmencita, *señorita*,' she answered, the wide dark eyes darting about the room. '*Puedo salir ahora?*'

Caroline sighed. She wasn't absolutely sure, but she

guessed Carmencita had orders not to gossip with the new governess, and spreading her hands, she gave her permission to leave.

With the door closed again she approached the tray with some misgivings. She would have preferred to go downstairs, to accustom herself to her new surroundings before she was summoned to meet her charge, but obviously she was obliged to follow orders. So she lifted the silver cloches that protected hot rolls and scrambled eggs, tasted the peach preserve, and poured herself some rich black coffee into a cup of such fine china it was virtually transparent.

Then, summoning all her composure, she opened her door and let herself into the corridor outside. The night before, Consuelo had escorted her to her room, bidden by Luis de Montejo, after his brother's undignified departure. Whatever his position in the house, his word appeared to carry as much weight as that of Don Esteban, and Caroline suspected that they respected him more. Two brothers could hardly have been more different, yet the result was the same. And did it really matter to these people?

The long hall stretched ahead of her, its stonework inlaid with panels of carving, and interspersed with portraits of long-dead Montejos. Overhead, the ceiling was an arch of heavily embossed moulding, and because it was without windows, it was constantly lit by a series of gothic sconces, each accommodating an electric bulb. It was curious, but the night before Caroline had scarcely been aware of its eerie isolation, those painted eyes in their canvas sockets troubling her not at all. But this morning, the remoteness of her rooms from the rest of the *hacienda* seemed infinitely significant, and she could not dispel the realisation that she was completely without support here.

She hurried along the corridor, her heels silent on the

softly piled carpet that unrolled its length in shades of black and gold, and emerged at the head of the staircase with a feeling of having navigated a particularly treacherous expanse of ocean.

Thinking of the nearness of the ocean, she endeavoured to dismiss her foolish fears. She was allowing the house, and its lavish appointments, to influence her impressions of her employer, and the sooner she found a true perspective the better.

Downstairs she encountered some of the servants, already at work, polishing the massive width of the hall on bended knees. They looked up curiously as she hesitated, uncertain as to her destination, and then the sound of a child's laughter erased the last traces of her irresolution. Nothing was more delightful than the spontaneous laughter of a child, she thought, crossing the hall in the direction of the voices she could now hear. Don Esteban must hold some affection in his daughter's eyes at least, and she was relieved to have the burden of indecision lifted from her.

But when she reached the arched doorway that led into a huge, sunlit *salón*, she faltered once again. Sure enough, her charge was there, a small, plump little girl, extravagantly arrayed in a white dress with layer upon layer of frills, overset by strings of pink ribbon, but the man who was on all fours, and on whose back she was energetically riding, was not her father.

'Ah, Miss Leyton! Good morning!'

With a lithe effort Luis de Montejo swung the child down from his back and got easily to his feet, quelling the little girl's protests with a soothing hand on her long black hair. In the same linen trousers he had worn the night before, but this time a cream silk shirt to complement them, he was relaxed and magnetic, a vibrant masculine being, with the unmistakable glow of good health. His shirt had become partially unbuttoned during his antics on the floor, and now his long fingers probed to fasten it, but not before Caroline had observed the dark arrowing of fine body hair that disappeared below his belt.

'Tio Vincente, Tio Vincente!' Emilia, for this was evidently Don Estaban's daughter, tugged impotently at his sleeve. '*Quien es?*' she exclaimed, subjecting Caroline to a malevolent scrutiny from beneath dark brows. '*Que desea? Ella no me gusta!*'

'Hush, little one. Speak in English, remember?' Luis exhorted her softly, restraining her sulky tirade. 'Miss Leyton is here to teach you your numbers, as you know very well. And I do not wish to hear that you have been rude to her.'

Emilia's lips pursed. 'I know my numbers,' she declared, in perfect English, surprising Caroline by her lack of accent. 'Miss Thackeray taught me my numbers, and my letters, and I do not need any more teachers.'

Miss Thackeray? Caroline's brow furrowed. Had Miss Thackeray been her predecessor, and if so, why was she no longer here?

'Miss Thackeray used to be my governess,' Luis inserted, dryly, correctly interpreting Caroline's little frown. 'She lived at San Luis from the time I was six years old, but unfortunately she died last year, and since then Emilia has had no formal education.'

'I see.' Caroline endeavoured to hide her relief. For an awful moment she wondered if she was the last in a succession of governesses, all of whom had objected to living at the *hacienda*.

'You won't like it here at San Luis,' Emilia stated now, abandoning her pleas to her uncle and turning instead to the offensive. 'There are snakes, and spiders, and bats that suck your blood!' She twisted her face into a horrifying grimace. 'Do you believe in vampires, Miss Leyton? Because if you do not, you must be as stupid as you look!' And brushing past Caroline, she ran out of the room, before either her governess or her uncle could prevent her.

'Well——' Left alone once again with Luis, Caroline felt hopelessly embarrassed, as much by her own sense of inadequacy as by what the child had said. 'What do I do now?'

Luis's mouth compressed. 'You are asking me?'

'Who else?' Caroline made an encompassing gesture around the otherwise empty room. 'There is no one else.' She expelled her breath unevenly. 'Is she always like that?'

Luis shrugged, tucking his thumbs into the back of his belt. 'You must make allowances for Emilia. She has had a rather—unusual upbringing.'

'That I can believe!' Caroline was vehement.

'Do not misunderstand me, Miss Leyton. I am not saying that Emilia is without—gentleness, compassion. Only that she has never known a mother's care.'

Caroline shook her head. 'But your aunt——'

'Tia Isabel is—how shall I say it?—a little unworldly.' He paused. 'Miss Thackeray provided the fulcrum of Emilia's existence. When she died . . .'

'But what about her father?' Caroline had to say it. 'Surely he——' She broke off, and then said inconsequently: 'For two brothers, you are totally different.'

'Forgive me,' Luis's grey eyes narrowed, 'but is that one of your famous English *non sequiturs*? I do not see what relevance it has to the purpose.'

'It hasn't,' Caroline sighed forlornly, bending her head. 'I mean, it has no relevance, of course. I just wish——' She broke off again. 'Are there really vampire bats here?'

Luis's mouth softened a little. 'And if I say yes, will you go running back to Merida?'

He was teasing her, but she could not respond to it. 'Perhaps, if I could,' she answered now, and his sudden humour disappeared behind a mask of gravity.

'I think I must be going,' he said, moving purposefully towards the door. 'I promised Tomas I would ride with him this morning, and it grows late.'

'Wait——' Caroline went after him urgently, her green eyes wide and anxious. 'Please, you have to tell me—what am I do do about Emilia? Where is she? When do her lessons begin? And—and are we allowed to go outside the grounds of the *hacienda*?'

Luis halted in the doorway and looked down at her with studied consideration. His stillness disturbed her. The penetration of those light eyes was disruptive. Her lungs began to feel constricted, and her throat felt tight, and she wondered if this was how a penitent felt in the presence of a confessor.

'I suggest you ask my brother these things,' he advised her at last, his voice curiously constrained. 'He is your employer, *señorita*, not I. Now, if you will permit me——'

'You're not—*leaving*!'

It seemed imperative that she should know this for a fact, and without really thinking what she was doing, she emulated Emilia's example and gripped his sleeve. Only somehow her fingers encountered the hair-roughened skin of his forearm, and the feeling of the taut muscle beneath his skin caused an involuntary tremor of awareness to ripple over her. She looked down at her fingers, spreading them almost experimentally, then her chin jerked upward as he wrenched his arm out of her grasp.

'I return to Mariposa in three days, *señorita*,' he told her harshly, and without another word, he strode away.

Caroline turned back into the *salón*, aware that she was trembling. She realised she had done an unforgivable thing by making him aware of her like that, but it had happened completely without her volition. Yet perhaps it was inevitable. He was the only person she could turn to, and she dreaded the thought of his eventual departure. But somehow she had to face that reality, and live with it.

'*Señorita!*'

For a moment, the whispered use of her name confused her. She had thought herself alone in the room. But now she saw that the door to an inner *salón* had opened, and a tiny figure, voluminous in folds of black silk, was hovering on the threshold. A headdress, of the kind Caroline had previously only seen on those ancient portraits upstairs, formed a kind of jewelled halo above the woman's coiled hair, and her ears and the gnarled knuckles of her fingers glittered with a veritable fortune in diamonds, rubies and emeralds.

'Doña Isabel?' ventured Caroline nervously, at a loss to know how else to address her, and the tiny figure bobbed her head in assent. 'How—how do you do? I'm Caroline Leyton—er—Emilia's new governess.'

'Governess, pah!' Doña Isabel released her hold on the door and advanced a few paces into the room, staring at Caroline with unconcealed contempt. 'I know who you are, *señorita*,' she admonished her, in a low guttural undertone. 'You are Esteban's latest *puta*, that is who you are! Do you think you can deceive me? I have lived here too long!'

Caroline was astounded. Her knowledge of Spanish might not be comprehensive, but she knew exactly what *puta* meant, and its connotations were not only shocking but insulting.

'I assure you, Doña Isabel——' she began, only to have the old lady interrupt her.

'Be silent! I do not hold conversations with *putas*!' she hissed arrogantly. 'How dare you enter my sister's sitting room? How dare you show your legs, like any common——'

'That will do, Tia Isabel.' The cultivated masculine tones came as such a relief that Caroline turned to face her employer with real gratitude in her face. She was fast coming to the conclusion that no one could remain sane

in this madhouse, and to see Don Esteban entering the
room, apparently composed, and sober, in his elegant
grey lounge suit, seemed almost a miracle.

'*Puta! Puta!*' cried Doña Isabel shrilly, her voice rising
in her agitation. 'How dare Esteban permit his women to
use my sister's——'

'Tia Isabel, my father is dead,' declared Don Esteban
flatly, spreading his hands apologetically in Caroline's
direction. '*Senorita*, please forgive my aunt. She is sometimes—forgetful.'

Caroline shook her head in bewilderment as the old
lady frowned, and tried to absorb what her nephew was
saying. 'Esteban is dead?' she echoed, thin brows meeting
above a long aquiline nose. 'Then—then who is this girl?
What is she doing at San Luis de Merced?'

'Miss Leyton is Emilia's new governess,' explained her
nephew calmly. 'You remember? I told you. She has
come from England to teach Emilia geography and history, *no*?'

Doña Isabel viewed Caroline with suspicion. 'But she
was here, talking with Luis. I saw the way she looked at
him!'

'You are imagining things, *mi tia*,' Esteban retorted,
evidently losing patience. 'Go back to your embroidery,
tia, I wish to discuss business matters with Miss Leyton.'

Doña Isabel hesitated, but clearly Esteban had the
upper hand, and with a gesture that was curiously pathetic she disappeared out the door through which she had
entered. Her departure was a definite relief, and Caroline
linked her fingers together in an effort to hide their obvious trembling, wishing she had more experience in these
matters.

'Please sit down.' Esteban was all sympathetic affability
now. 'I do not know how I can satisfactorily atone for my
aunt's behaviour, except to beg your indulgence for her
temporary lapses of memory.' He sighed. 'She is—was—

my mother's sister, an unmarried lady of uncertain years, and prone, I regret to say, to periods of fantasy concerning my father's behaviour.'

Caroline, who had subsided gratefully on to a satin-striped sofa, looked up at him. 'You mean your father is the Esteban she talks about?'

'That is correct. I was named for him.'

'I see,' Caroline nodded.

'And of course, Isabel was a little jealous of her sister's good fortune.' He smiled, showing even white teeth, brilliant in his dark face. 'Is it not always the way with unmarried ladies?'

Caroline made an awkward gesture, not quite knowing how to answer him, and taking advantage of her momentary confusion, he came down on to the sofa beside her, his bulk causing the cushions to slope a little in his direction.

'*Señorita!*' He looked diffident, and for a moment she thought he was going to apologise for his own behaviour the night before, but he didn't. '*Señorita*, I am so glad you have come here. Emilia—my daughter, you understand—is sorely in need of young companionship. I do not know how much Doña Elena—Señora Garcia, that is—told you, but since my wife's death, Emilia has been brought up by an elderly countrywoman of yours, a Miss Thackerary.'

'Yes.' Caroline acknowledged this, without explaining how she was so informed, and he went on eagerly:

'She was not a good influence on the child, *señorita*. Many times, she went against my judgment in matters concerning Emilia, and unfortunately my brother Luis took her part.'

'I see.' This was deeper water. 'I'm sorry.'

'So am I.' Esteban was grave. 'Luis and I are brothers, and it is always sad when blood turns against blood.'

'Oh, I'm sure——' began Caroline awkwardly, only to

break off abruptly when Esteban raised his hand.

'You do not yet understand, Miss Leyton. Just as Tia Isabel was jealous of her sister, so Luis is jealous of me.'

'No——'

'But yes. I regret so.' And indeed, Esteban did look melancholy. 'I am the elder brother, *entiende*? I have inherited our father's estate. Luis has nothing, except what I give him. His mother, you see, was the *puta* of whom Tia Isabel speaks.'

Caroline's face felt frozen in an attitude of disbelief, and as if realising he had gone too far, Esteban hastened to retract.

'Forgive me,' he said, as she shrank back against the cushions. 'I should not have told you so brutally. I do not mean to be—callous, but I cannot forget that it was Luis's mother who caused my mother's death. She killed herself, you know, *mi madre*. She flung herself from a second floor window down to the courtyard beneath.' He massaged his temples with the middle finger and the thumb of one hand. 'Believe me, that is not something one can easily forget.'

'But——' Caroline swallowed convulsively, 'your—your brother's name is Montejo.'

'Oh, yes.' Esteban heaved a heavy sigh. 'My father married Luis's mother—afterwards. My brother is no bastard, *señorita*. At least,' he paused, 'he is not illegitimate.'

CHAPTER THREE

CAROLINE and her charge were to work in the library.

After unburdening himself of the reasons for the anti-pathy between himself and Luis, Esteban became calm and businesslike. With a sense of pride, in complete contrast to his inconsequence of the night before, he showed Caroline around the main rooms of the *hacienda*, pointing out particular pieces of interest, and relating a little of their history. He was knowledgeable about the myths and legends of the area, making her blood tingle with stories of mindless clay men created by the gods, of soulless wooden men whose tools rose up in rebellion against them, and who were turned into monkeys. He showed her an Aztec funerary mask, and described how the evil goddess Tezcatlipoca had dressed the god Quetzalcoatl in such a mask before forcing him to take part in a drunken orgy of lust and incest. The culmination had been that Quetzalcoatl had flung himself on a funeral pyre, and after several days of purification, his heart had risen to the heavens to become the planet Venus.

There were many such legends, each attached to some remnant of history. As well as the overwhelming influence of Catholicism, there were also tiny effigies of Totec, the Mayan god of mankind; Yum Caax, the maize god; Kinich Ahau and Tlacolteutl; Xolotl, Quetzalcoatl's brother, and Hanhau, the Mayan god of death. The *hacienda* was a treasure house of gold and antiquity, and although there was something slightly vulgar about it, it was undeniably impressive.

It was while they were examining the *azulejos* in the music room that Caroline became aware of someone

41

watching them, and turning quickly, she saw Emilia hovering reluctantly in the doorway. Esteban turned and saw her, too, and with a gesture of welcome bade her join them.

'Come, *pequeña*,' he beckoned her affably. 'Come and meet Miss Leyton. She is your new governess, and I want you to be friends.'

Emilia made no move towards them. Clearly, Esteban had not been lying when he said she disobeyed him, but whether that was through Luis's influence or not, there was no way of knowing—yet. Certainly Luis's affection for the little girl had seemed genuine enough, and hers for him, but until Caroline had had a chance to talk with her she could make no real assessment.

'Emilia! *Venga! Inmediatamente!*' Esteban's voice had lost a lot of its benevolence. 'Come—see what I have here for you.' He fumbled in his pocket, as if searching for a gift. 'If you do not come and look, you will never know what it is I have here, will you? Now, are you going to do as you are told?'

Emilia sighed, and then, evidently curious to know what he was holding, she left her position by the door and approached them with measured steps. She scarcely looked at Caroline. Her attention was all concentrated on her father, and as she neared him she tilted her head slightly, trying to see what he had in his hand.

Caroline was curious, too, but she stepped aside politely, unwilling to intrude on this exchange between father and daughter. It was the first time she had seen them together, but although there was a faint family resemblance, Emilia's features must more closely resemble those of her mother.

What happened next happened so suddenly, it was over before she could protest, even had she dared to do so. As Emilia stretched out her neck to glimpse what her father was holding, his hand shot out and caught her, biting into her arm with cruel intent, as his other hand delivered a blow to her cheek. Emilia staggered, and would have fallen had he not been holding her. Her face went white, as white as the muslin of her dress, except for the livid marks of her father's fingers that were rapidly reddening, but she did not cry. Caroline could see her steeling herself, forcing back the tears, and realised, as the blood drained from her own face, that she was holding her own breath.

She expelled it as Don Esteban caught his daughter's chin between his fingers, forcing her face up to his. 'Let that be a lesson to you, *pequeña*,' he declared, with cold emphasis. 'You will not make a fool of me in front of Miss Leyton, as you tried to do with Miss Thackeray!'

'No, *señor*.'

Emilia spoke respectfully, but her voice was sullen. It was obvious from her behaviour that this was not the first time her father had struck her, but she had learned from experience not to answer back.

'Now, greet Miss Leyton as the daughter of the house of Montejo should do, with politeness and courtesy, and a smile on that sulky little face of yours,' he advised, and Caroline had to face yet another mortifying moment.

'Welcome to San Luis de Merced, Miss Leyton,' Emilia recited, her eyes downcast. And then, at her father's insistence, she lifted her head and spread her lips in an unholy rictus. 'I hope you will be very happy here.'

Caroline gathered herself with difficulty. 'Thank you, Emilia,' she replied stiffly. 'I—hope I will be, too.'

'So, now the formalities are over, we will show Miss Leyton where you are to work,' announced Don Esteban, releasing his daughter's arm. 'I think you will find my choice of venue appealing, Miss Leyton. The library is a soundproof room, and I have many interesting first editions.'

The library was as impressive as the rest of the house. Books lined the walls from floor to ceiling, leather-bound and highly polished, their gold lettering as distinctive now as it had ever been.

'As you can see, I insist that this collection must be kept in perfect condition,' Esteban said proudly. 'From time to time, I have an expert come here from the university in Mexico City. He examines the books, and arranges any restorative work that is necessary.'

Caroline looked round her in admiration. A tiny, iron-railed balcony was situated near the moulded ceiling, enabling any enthusiastic bibliophile access to the upper shelves, and a delicately carved spiral staircase complemented the mobile ladder that provided a means of reaching the volumes out of reach.

'You will work here.' Esteban indicated a leather-topped desk, set beneath the long windows. 'See—I have arranged for Emilia's books to be placed here for your perusal, and if you require anything further, it can be obtained from the supplier in Merida.'

'Thank you.' Caroline touched the pile of worn text-books with a grateful finger. This, at least, was something she knew and understood, and she glanced anxiously at Emilia, expecting to meet resentment or antagonism. But Emilia returned her gaze with only faintly hostile eyes, and Caroline's spirits lifted slightly at the prospect of making some headway.

'I will leave you,' Esteban said now, much to her relief. 'I have matters of the estate to discuss, with my overseer. I will see you both at lunchtime, *señorita*, when we can discuss Emilia's progress. Until then, *hasta luego*, Miss Leyton. *Hasta luego*, Emilia.'

The door closed, and Caroline sank down rather weakly on to the leather chair beside the desk. The silence that followed Esteban's departure was pregnant with emotion, but anything was better than the tension that had gripped her since Emilia joined them in the music room.

Emilia moved round the desk now, to lean with her elbows on its surface. She regarded Caroline's troubled face with concentration for a few moments, and then, with an inconsequence mature for her years, she said: 'I told you you wouldn't like it here.'

Caroline looked at her blankly, then briskly reached for one of the dog-eared textbooks. 'You know, you could be right,' she remarked calmly, and opened the book.

'You didn't tell him,' Emilia went on insistently. 'You didn't tell Don Esteban what I said. Why not?'

'What you said?' Caroline frowned, as if she couldn't remember the child's words in intimate detail. 'What did you say?'

Emilia sighed. 'You know! About your not liking it here. About the spiders and the vampires!'

'Oh, I see.' Caroline shrugged her slim shoulders. 'I'd forgotten. Besides, of what interest would that be to your father?'

'Don't call him that!' exclaimed Emilia fiercely. 'He's not my father! I hate him!'

'Emilia!' Caroline had to protest now. 'He is your father, and you shouldn't say such things about him. It— well, it's rude, and ignorant.'

Emilia straightened. 'Tio Vincente is my father,' she declared, causing Caroline's lips to part in stunned disbelief. Was there no end to the revelations she was to be subjected to? 'Tio Vincente loved my mother. That's why Don Esteban hates me.'

'Oh, don't be so silly, Emilia.' Caroline had had enough for one day. 'Look, I'm not here to discuss who might or might not have loved your mother. I'm sure your father cared for her very deeply, and just because you're disobedient, and your father punishes you, there's no reason for you to go spreading malicious tales that have no basis in fact. You're your father's daughter—it's obvious! Now, sit down, and stop behaving like a melo-dramatic two-year-old.'

Emilia pursed her lips. 'You don't know anything.'

'Nor do I want to,' retorted Caroline shortly, un-comfortably aware that her motives for feeling that way were not entirely disinterested. She couldn't help re-membering Luis's reticence when she had asked about Emilia's mother's death, and his reluctance to discuss his brother's reaction. But, as she had continually to keep telling herself, the personal affairs of the Montejos were nothing to do with her, and she determinedly began to ask Emilia questions, in an attempt to assess the child's capabilities.

In fact, the morning passed quite quickly. Once she became interested in proving what a bright and intelli-gent pupil she was, Emilia lost that air of antagonistic aggression, and showed an entirely more sympathetic side to her nature. She was sharp and intelligent, and al-though Luis had told her that Miss Thackeray had died last year, her education was far in advance of most chil-dren of that age. She read well, and with expression, and her mental arithmetic was good. If she had a failing, it was that she was sometimes too quick with her answers, and in consequence made careless mistakes that given a little more time, she would have avoided. She had obvi-ously enjoyed her lessons with Miss Thackeray, and what-ever the old lady's failings, so far as Emilia's education was concerned, she had done a good job.

Emilia told her that lunch was usually served at one o'clock, so at half past twelve Caroline dismissed her pupil. She had decided to return to her room and do some of her unpacking, as well as attending to her ap-pearance. But when she opened the door to her apart-ments, she found that someone had forestalled her, and her clothes had all been hung away and her cases stowed in the closet. Unused to such assiduous attention, Caroline felt somewhat disconcerted, but a swift examination of the drawers and wardrobe assured her that her belongings had been handled with the utmost care and consideration.

Examining her reflection in the dressing table mirror, she noted the faint flush that still lingered in her cheeks, a reminder of the disturbing morning she had spent, she brushed a pale powder compound across the revealing colour in an attempt to disguise her agitation, then re-applied the lip-gloss to her mouth. In truth, she did feel a little hungry now, having refused a cup of chocolate mid-morning, but the prospect of seeing Luis again, after his brother's revelations, tightened the muscles of her throat.

She traversed the length of the corridor again, and descended the stairs at ten minutes to one, only to encounter the subject of her nervous speculations in the hall. Luis had evidently just come in from riding, for he was wearing black leather gaucho pants and an open-necked black shirt, and the scent of horseflesh was unmistakable as he moved to pass her and climb the stairs.

'I trust you have had an enjoyable morning, *señorita*,' he remarked, with his innate courtesy, and Caroline knew an hysterical desire to laugh in his face. *An enjoyable morning!* If he only knew, she thought wildly, then composed herself to reply quietly: 'It was most interesting, *señor*. And you?'

Luis paused, two stairs up, arrested by her conventional response. 'I enjoy riding,' he said, after a moment's consideration. 'You must try it while you are here. Esteban keeps a good stable.' And without giving her a chance to make any further comment, he mounted the rest of the stairs, two at a time.

Caroline sauntered across the hall, unsure what to do, or where to go. The *salón*, where Doña Isabel had accosted her earlier, was empty, and breathing a little more freely, she moved across to the windows.

From here, it was possible to see the forecourt, and the sweep of formal gardens away to the left. Within the high walls of the fortress-like building were manicured lawns and flower beds, and a carefully pruned row of fruit trees, espaliered against the stone, softening its grim exterior. A means of escape? reflected Caroline dryly, then turned as footsteps sounded behind her.

'There you are, Miss Leyton.' Her employer stood framed in the arch of the open doorway, correct and businesslike in his pale grey attire. Aside from the fact that he was smaller than his brother, and stockier, his features were not so finely chiselled, and his tongue appeared to moisten his thick lips as he took in the delightful picture she made. With the sun behind her, her hair was like a pale aureole around her head, and he held out his hand encouragingly, urging her to join him. 'Lunch is an informal meal at San Luis, *señorita*,' he added gently. 'I will show you how we help ourselves.'

Taking a deep breath, Caroline crossed the *salón* again to join him, and his hand lightly cupped her elbow. 'I hope you had no trouble with Emilia after I left, *señorita*,' he exhorted her, as they passed through the hall, and Caroline squashed the desire to release herself from his grasp, and assured him that his daughter had been an exemplary pupil.

'This is good,' he exclaimed, obviously pleased. 'For too long, she has had no kind of discipline. I hope you will understand me when I say I expect your support in all things, and——' he paused, fingering his tie, 'that you will remember that it is I, and no one else, who gives you your instructions.'

His meaning was unmistakable, and Caroline's lips tightened. 'Of course, *señor*,' she murmured, stifling her protests, and her employer permitted a self-satisfied smile.

Esteban escorted her to the morning room. It was not the room where they had eaten the night before, and was much less ornate than most of the rooms in the *hacienda*. Exquisitely-embroidered tapestries took the place of elaborate panelling, and predominantly turquoise and gold in design, they kept the room light and airy. Now, long french doors had been opened on to a sunlit terrace, where an arched colonnade provided shade for long buffet tables, and Caroline could not suppress the gasp of pleasure that escaped her when she saw the dappled waters beyond. A patio, chequered with mosaic, surrounded the sunken pool, and a realistically poised jaguar was frozen in an attitude of menace, while a crystal-clear fountain cascaded from its jaws.

'*Patio del Jaguar!*' announced Esteban, with a flourish. 'A fitting background for the lion of San Luis, would you not agree?' he prompted, and Caroline, who was slightly disconcerted by this display of conceit, hid her misgivings in a projected show of admiration.

'The jaguar,' she exclaimed effusively, 'he looks so real!' And she escaped his oppressive possession by stepping out into the brilliant sunshine.

Until then she had not appreciated how hot it really was. The thick walls of the *hacienda* provided their own brand of air-conditioning, and until she felt the sun beating down on her head, she had felt reasonably cool. Now, she lifted her face almost worshipfully to the sun, and pressed her hands to the back of her neck. It was a gesture of unconscious sensuality, but she was unaware of it, until her attention was caught by a movement at an upper window. Almost against her will, her eyes were locked for a brief moment with Luis's, then he drew back out of sight, and she was left with the awareness of Don Esteban's brooding appraisal. Immediately her hands dropped to her sides, and relinquishing her desire to explore further, she returned to the terrace.

'You are a sun-worshipper, Miss Leyton?' Esteban enquired, his voice thicker than she remembered it, and she forced a light smile.

'I—I didn't realise it was so hot,' she confessed. 'What a pity one can't swim in the pool.'

'That could be arranged,' Esteban remarked, his eyes lingering on the burgeoning curve of her breast, but Caroline chose to ignore him, as she turned determinedly to the buffet tables.

A mouthwatering display of dishes awaited their attention. Various salads, and their attendant sauces, flanked curried eggs and creamy stuffed avocadoes; shellfish, served in their own shells; cold meats and gelatines, and chilled fruit juices. For the more adventurous, there were steaming *enchiladas*, and *tacos*, dishes of fried chicken, and bowls of *chili con carne*, which Caroline knew from experience was nothing like the *chili con carne* she had had at home, and delicious caramel desserts, nestling in beds of fresh peaches and apricots.

Esteban encouraged her to try the *tortillas*, but Caroline chose a chicken salad, and she was seated on the terrace, a glass of chilled white wine in her hand, when Luis and Emilia joined them.

'Ah, *chica*,' exclaimed Esteban, beckoning his daughter towards him, apparently indifferent to his attitude to her earlier, and wary of his uncertain temper, the child approached.

Someone had washed her face and brushed her long dark hair, and the frilly white dress had been replaced by an equally unsuitable pink one, with long lace sleeves, that must be quite restraining in the heat, Caroline suspected. A slight bruise on her cheekbone was all that remained of the blow her father had delivered earlier, but Caroline guessed it was tender, and flinched when Esteban flicked it with a careless finger.

'Let that be a lesson to you, Emilia,' he admonished

her lightly. 'You are to do exactly as Miss Leyton tells you, and I expect to hear that she has no further trouble with you.'

'Yes, *señor*.' Emilia glanced at Caroline from beneath her dark lashes, and glimpsing the rekindled hostility, Caroline could have wished her employer had chosen less ambiguous words. Did Emilia think she had been complaining about her? Or did she imagine she had confessed her previous insolence? Either way, it was going to be a continuing struggle keeping Emilia and her father sweet, and she didn't honestly know if she wanted that responsibility. Then she encountered Luis's grey gaze, and knew that for good or ill she was already committed— although to what she had yet to discover.

Aside from the inherent disharmony among the participants, it was very pleasant eating lunch on the terrace. The sun filtering through the flowering vine cast moving shadows over the mellow stonework, and the shrubs spilling from their tubs around the pool dappled the monolithic stillness of the crouching predator. Insects buzzed among the flame trees, and exotically-patterned butterflies skimmed the falling bubbling fountain, adding the frantic flutter of their wings to the cooling effluence of the water.

Esteban was disposed to be affable, and although Luis entered the conversation only rarely, those occasions when his brother addressed him were not the fraught offensives of the night before. On the contrary, they discussed the estate and its problems, and if sometimes Esteban's contempt for his brother's more democratic methods of running the *hacienda* surfaced, he quickly disguised it, beneath a mask of urbanity. Perhaps he wanted to show he could be tolerant, too, Caroline reflected, tense in spite of herself when Luis chose to argue.

Emilia, after attracting her father's initial attention, took no part in the conversation at all, spending her time feeding small pieces of meat to the white doves that flew down from the cupola above their heads. She was evidently accustomed to her father's variable moods, and Caroline knew a sudden sympathy for her. It could not be easy, living here without friends or companions, and she determined to try and show her how to play as well as work.

The meal over, a black-clad nursemaid appeared to take Emilia away for her *siesta*, and taking the opportunity presented when one of Esteban's servants came to speak to him, Caroline, too, made her escape. She needed time to herself, she decided, time to assimilate her position here so far, and with a feeling of weariness out of all proportion to the amount of work she had accomplished, she made her way up to her room.

With the blinds drawn, it was very cool and pleasant lying on her bed, and she relaxed almost instinctively. Perhaps it was not going to be so bad as she had at first thought, she thought sleepily, and lost consciousness before her brain had time to examine the things she had learned.

She awakened a couple of hours later, feeling considerably refreshed. When she released the blinds, the shadows were longer, and in the distance, the sea had a distinctly amber tinge. She longed to be near the sea, to plunge into its cool waters and dispel the sticky aftermath of her nap, but as that was not possible, she went and took another shower.

Afterwards, she dressed in cream cotton trousers and a loose embroidered smock, with wide elbow-length sleeves. She would have preferred to wear a cotton vest, and leave her slim arms bare, but the outfit seemed too immodest in the confines of the *hacienda*. Besides, she had no desire to give Don Esteban the wrong impression, and after brushing her hair and restoring a light make-up, she left her room in search of a cool drink.

The *hacienda* seemed very quiet as she made her way

downstairs, her sandalled feet echoing hollowly as she crossed the wide tiled hall. There was no one in either of the *salóns* she entered, and the library was equally deserted, the french doors in the morning room closed now, the buffet tables removed. She was hesitating over whether to summon one of the servants when the door to a small anteroom she had noticed earlier opened, and Luis Montejo appeared. He seemed deep in thought, his head bent and his dark brows drawn closely together, but when he saw her he transferred his hands to his pockets, regarding her presence with polite but distant enquiry.

'*Señorita*,' he observed courteously, inclining his head. 'Are you looking for my brother, or Emilia? I should tell you, Esteban is resting, and would not welcome being disturbed, and Emilia does not take lessons in the afternoon.'

Caroline pressed her lips together. 'As—as a matter of fact, I was hoping I might be able to get a glass of cold water. Consuelo advised me not to drink the water from the taps upstairs.'

'She was correct.' Luis frowned. 'In any case, the tanks become warm and the water is unpleasantly tepid. However,' he paused, 'you may have something more appetising, if you prefer. There is a refrigerated cabinet in Esteban's study, containing various kinds of fruit sodas. Perhaps you would like one of them, instead of cold water.'

Caroline hesitated. 'But won't your brother——'

'Esteban will never notice,' Luis assured her, with a curious twist to his mouth, and led the way along a corridor, similar to the one upstairs. Only this time the portraits were interspersed with narrow, fluted-glass windows, and the carpet underfoot was in shades of red and silver.

Esteban had not shown her his study during their morning tour, but now Luis led the way into a room only slightly smaller than the library. As in the library, there were shelves of files and books, mostly agricultural tomes, she noticed, and an imposing square desk, set with two dark green telephones. The desk was neat and tidy, however, with no outstanding piles of papers waiting attention, and Caroline decided that Esteban was either extremely efficient—or extremely bored.

She chose a lime-juice cordial from the drinks cabinet, then arched her brows when Luis took nothing. 'Won't you join me?' she asked, reluctant to be left to her own devices again, but the tall dark Mexican shook his head.

'I regret I do not have the time, *señorita*,' he demurred politely, following her out of the room and closing the door. 'But I have no doubt Esteban would not object if you chose to walk in the gardens, or borrowed one of the books from the library.'

Caroline looked up at him mutinously, making no effort to open the ring-pull can. 'I wanted to talk to you,' she exclaimed, stung by his indifference, and his expression hardened as he met her resentful eyes.

'I am sure if you have any questions, my brother will be happy to answer them,' he said, hooking his thumbs into his belt. 'I hear that he approves of your behaviour so far, and I am sure Emilia can only benefit from your example.'

Caroline pursed her lips. 'I don't want to talk to Don Esteban,' she declared, in a low tone, 'I want to talk to you. I—I wanted to apologise for what happened——'

'There is no need.' He interrupted her harshly, waving away her attempt at conciliation. 'I am glad to have been of service, *señorita*. And now, I have work to attend to.'

Caroline heaved a sigh, then, before he could take too many steps away from her, she hastened after him. '*Señor! Señor*, you said I might be able to ride while I was here: could I do so now? Emilia doesn't need me, as you said, and I'm not in the mood for reading.'

Luis's lean dark face was intent. '*Señorita*, you cannot ride alone—surely you realise that? Aside from the evident dangers, a woman does not go out unescorted, and I suggest you discuss the matter with my brother, and ascertain his opinion.'

Caroline gazed up at him frustratedly, brushing back her hair with an impatient hand. 'You mean—I'm a prisoner here, is that it? I'm not allowed outside the hacienda without a prison escort!'

'You are over-dramatising the situation, *señorita*,' Luis exclaimed heavily, glancing about him as if hoping for a distraction. 'I am sure that something will be arranged, if you request it. Who knows, maybe *el patrón* himself will accompany you. Even though it may result in your having to ride in the carriage.'

'The carriage?' Caroline echoed blankly, and Luis sighed.

'My brother does not ride, *señorita*,' he retorted flatly. 'But he may be persuaded to make an exception in your case.'

Caroline caught her lower lip between her teeth, biting hard. 'I don't want your brother to escort me,' she burst out impetuously. 'And if you won't take me, then I shall find some way to go alone——'

'You will not!' He overrode her declaration with harsh admonition. 'Be assured, *señorita*, I shall inform Esteban, if you do attempt to do so, and it may very well result in your forfeiting any opportunity in the future.'

Caroline gasped. 'You'd do that?' She shook her head. 'You brought me here! Doesn't that give you any sense of responsibility at all?'

'I did not bring you here, *señorita*,' he contradicted her forcefully. 'I transported you the few miles from Las Estadas, that is all. You applied for this job, *you* accepted the appointment, and *you* travelled all these miles, at the instigation of Señora Garcia, to take up the position. How can you blame me if it is not wholly to your liking?'

Looking into his grim face, Caroline wondered how she had had the nerve to say what she had. But it was said now, and she could not retract it. So she stood her ground, facing him a little uncertainly, and summoning her courage to go on.

'But you didn't warn me what to expect, did you?' she accused him recklessly. 'You didn't tell me that your brother liked inflicting pain, or that your aunt was likely to insult me——'

'Tia Isabel insulted you? How did she do that?'

Caroline shook her head. 'She—she accused me of being one of—one of your father's——'

'I understand.' Luis held up his hand to silence her, his face twisting impatiently. 'Did you tell Esteban?'

'He knew,' said Caroline dully, feeling a headache beginning to probe at her temples. 'He was there.' She sighed. 'Oh, what does it matter? You don't really care about me. Just so long as Emilia doesn't suffer.'

Luis watched her as she walked away from him, her head bent, her silky hair falling at either side of her face, exposing the vulnerable nape of her neck. Then he muttered angrily to himself, before going after her.

'Tomorrow morning,' he said harshly as he passed her, scarcely slowing his stride. 'At six o'clock, *señorita*. I shall be waiting in the hall.'

CHAPTER FOUR

PERHAPS because she had slept during the heat of the day, Caroline found it hard to sleep that night. Although her room was dark and cool, her thoughts were hot and excited, and she tossed about restlessly on the softly-sprung mattress, unable to find a comfortable place to relax.

Even without the restricting influence of the sheet, her skin felt moist and prickly, and her heart seemed to be beating unnaturally loud.

She determinedly turned her mind to thoughts of home, realising that apart from a card from Merida, she had not yet written to her parents. Tomorrow she would have to try and find the time to compose a letter, and hope that the strangeness of her surroundings would not be discernible from her descriptions. In spite of her own misgivings, she didn't want her parents to worry, and her mother surely would, if she suspected the situation at San Luis.

It was harder to think of Andrew, but she did it, realising with a pang that she had scarcely thought of him all day. His image had receded, to be replaced by a darker, harder profile, with the long straight nose and finely moulded lips of the ascetic. Luis de Montejo! A man different from other men, yet just as disturbing to her peace of mind.

Thrusting his image aside also, she recalled Don Esteban's conversation that evening. Luis had not joined them for dinner, but Doña Isabel had, and Caroline had been uneasy, until it became apparent that the old lady was quite lucid this evening. Dressed in the inevitable black, but with a fine lace *mantilla* about her shoulders, and caught at the throat with an enormous diamond pin, she presided over the table with her nephew, occasionally subjecting Caroline to a not-unfriendly appraisal.

'Esteban tells me you are from London, *señorita*,' she observed, her somewhat clawlike fingers crumbling the roll on her plate. 'I went to London once, in 1946. I thought it was an ugly place, and it rained—all the time.'

'Tia Isabel, London was subjected to saturation bombing during the war,' Esteban inserted patiently. 'What you saw was the result of that desecration. I myself have been there since, and I can assure you it is not ugly.'

'Were you born in London, *señorita*?' Dona Isabel persisted, undaunted by her nephew's interruption, and Caroline shook her head.

'My family used to live just outside London, *señora*, in Buckinghamshire. But I attended university in London, and I know it very well.'

'Hah!' Doña Isabel nodded. 'And did your parents approve of this?'

Caroline frowned. 'Approve of what, *señora*?'

'Approve of you attending university, of course.' Doña Isabel shook her head. 'And travelling so far, without a *dueña*,' she added. 'When I was a girl, such things would never have been permitted.'

'Miss Leyton is a product of the twentieth century, *tia*,' Don Esteban interposed smoothly. 'And we should be grateful that she has chosen to come to San Luis, and be the companion Emilia needs.'

Doña Isabel pursed her lips. 'Emilia needs a mother's care,' she declared, nibbling at the tips of her fingers. 'Brother and sisters to bring her companionship.' She sighed. 'But with you a *viudo*, Esteban, and your brother destined for *la iglesia*, how can we hope for miracles?'

'I do not think Miss Leyton would agree with you,' Esteban retorted now. 'Emilia is not so unique.' He smiled at Caroline, his dark eyes warmly approving. 'And with the *señorita*'s assistance, we may all prosper.'

Caroline applied herself to the spicy mixture of rice and chicken on her plate, embarrassed by Don Esteban's unctuousness, and Doña Isabel shrugged her thin shoulders in dismissal.

'Perhaps;' she murmured, without conviction, and to Caroline's relief the subject was dropped.

No one questioned where Luis was, but while they were taking coffee in the *salón* later, his name again entered the conversation. It was Doña Isabel who introduced the subject, and Caroline's cheeks had burned during the old lady's disturbing exchange with her nephew.

'I saw that woman leaving the *hacienda* again this afternoon,' she announced irritably, clattering the fragile coffee cup in its saucer. 'I saw her leaving by the *puerta accesoria*. I will not have that woman in this house, Esteban! You must speak to Luis again!'

Her nephew looked slightly disconcerted by this unprovoked outburst, and his words in consequence were persuasively appeasing. 'Tia Isabel, *cara*, I do not think we need discuss this affair in front of Miss Leyton. I will speak to Luis, as you say, and the matter will be dealt with.'

'You have said that before, Esteban,' declared Doña Isabel peevishly, not prepared to surrender so easily. 'If Luis has need of a woman of that sort, why can he not arrange to meet her in the village?'

'Tia Isabel, I have told you, I will attend to it.' Don Esteban's eyes glittered ominously. 'What Luis chooses to do in his spare time is not Miss Leyton's concern, and I suggest you restrict your remarks to less personal matters.'

Caroline, in truth, was at a loss to know what to think. Who was this woman Doña Isabel spoke about? Some penitent of Luis's, here for him to hear her confession? Some poor creature dependent on him for charity? Or, more realistically, judging from the censure in Doña Isabel's voice, the kind of woman used for only one purpose, the idea of which caused a definitely hollow feeling in the pit of Caroline's stomach.

It was this, as much as anything, that was keeping her awake. She was disturbed by what she had heard, puzzled by the reasons behind it, and troubled by the awareness of her own involvement. Was that who Luis had been with when she saw him that afternoon? Was she the reason for that thoughtful expression he had been wearing? And was she, Caroline, by her persistence, an unwitting accessory to his deception of his brother?

Eventually she slept, only to awaken seemingly minutes later to an impatient tattoo at her door. Someone was knocking, determined to arouse her, and she struggled up on her pillows, groping for her watch.

It was six-fifteen, and scarcely light outside, but her heart pounded in sudden comprehension. It was Luis; it had to be. And scrambling off the bed, she sped across the room to the door.

'Who is it?' she breathed, her throat dry, and the constant tapping ceased.

'Montejo,' he said, with grim inflection. 'Have you changed your mind?'

'No! *No!*' Caroline spoke without hesitation, glancing behind her helplessly at the tumbled bed. 'Can—can you give me ten minutes? I've overslept. I promise I won't be long.'

'Five minutes,' he declared, delivering one last blow to the panels, and she heard his booted feet as he strode away down the corridor.

She sluiced her face and cleaned her teeth, contenting herself with the briefest of ablutions, and dressed without deliberation in purple jeans and cotton shirt. She wore boots instead of shoes, folding the legs of her jeans inside them, and snatched up a sweater as she went out the door. She didn't bother with make-up. Her skin was naturally pink from the haste with which she had readied herself, and her hair swung silkily about her cheeks as she hurried along the lamplit corridor.

Luis was waiting in the hall. She saw him as soon as she reached the landing, pacing restlessly about the black and gold tiling, flicking his knee-length black boots with the long muzzle of a rifle. The gun gave her pause, an unexpected weapon, in the hands of an expert, she was sure, as lean and dangerous as the man himself. Dressed in black, he exuded a lethal magnetism, and she realised how uncomplicated her relationship with Andrew had been, when compared to the feelings this man evoked in her.

He saw her as she started to descend, and his grey eyes narrowed speculatively. She was made uncomfortably aware that he did not consider jeans a suitable accoutrement to riding, but his words to her were impersonal, negating his unspoken reprobation.

'We will need to hurry if you are to see anything of the estate,' he said flatly, and without giving her time to reply he thrust open the door through which she had seen him entering the previous afternoon, and indicated that she should precede him.

Caroline found herself in a small cloakroom, with two further doors opening from it. The first was heavy and studded, with a crucifix nailed to its surface, but the other was the one Luis opened, giving access to the garden outside. Caroline licked her lips. This had to be the side door Doña Isabel had mentioned the night before. She had looked up *puerta accesoria* in her dictionary before going to bed, and she swallowed rather convulsively at the confirmation of the old lady's story, and the inevitable conclusions she had reached.

Outside, the air was incredibly fresh and sweet, and for a moment she forgot her apprehensions. Then Luis closed the door behind them and bade her follow him, and she hastened in his footsteps, aware of the sudden weight she felt upon her.

Luis had evidently made all the arrangements earlier, for his own mount and a soft-eyed chestnut mare were already saddled and waiting for them. The old Mexican stable-boy smiled benevolently as Luis took the time to thank him for his trouble, and proffered his hands for Caroline to use as a mounting block. After a brief glance at Luis, Caroline accepted his assistance, and he hoisted her firmly on to the chestnut's back.

It was easily four years since Caroline had ridden

a friend's pony, on a farm near her old home in Buckinghamshire, but the lessons she had learnt then still stood
her in good stead. The mare was much bigger than the
pony had been, of course, but she was docile and amen-
able, and after assuring himself that Caroline could
handle her, Luis swung himself on to the back of a dark
red gelding. He tucked the butt of the rifle into a leather
pocket attached to the front of his saddle, then said
something in Spanish to the grinning old man.

'*Desde luego, señor,*' he answered eagerly, and hastened
into the stables again, to reappear moments later with a
wide-brimmed sombrero. '*Por tu, señorita,*' he said, offering
it to Caroline, and meeting Luis's eyes again, she made
an involuntary little shrug as she took it.

'Never go riding without a hat,' he advised her softly,
and with a helpless gesture she jammed the well-worn
crown on to her head.

'*Mucha suerte, señorita, señor,*' exclaimed the old man
cheerfully, as they rode out of the yard, and Luis raised his
hand in farewell as he urged the horses forward.

Gomez came out to open the gates for them, and Luis
had a smile and a friendly word for him, too. Like the
stable-boy, Gomez evidently liked the younger Montejo,
and Caroline couldn't help wondering whether Esteban
inspired the same affection in his employees.

Beyond the gates, the ground sloped away steeply in a
series of gullies and shallow ravines, thick with shrubs and
trailing creepers. The lush vegetation had a primitive
beauty, but Caroline couldn't help remembering what
Emilia had said about snakes and spiders, and she felt
sure this was exactly the sort of habitat they would fre-
quent. She was relieved, therefore, when Luis did not ride
down the track towards the village, but branched off on a
circular route, that followed the walls of the *hacienda* for
some way, before giving naturally on to the gentler in-
cline that formed the northern boundary.

Given her head, the mare was quite happy to follow Luis's mount's example, and trotted obediently after the more spirited animal. But, as the shrubby undergrowth gave way to open grassland, the gelding quickened its pace, and Caroline had to concentrate to keep her seat, as the mare broke into a gallop. Yet it was stimulating, after all the tensions of the last couple of days, and she was glad that the cord of her hat was under her chin, when the wind caught the sombrero, tipping in on to her neck.

She was breathless and exhilarated when Luis finally slowed his mount, and the mare caught up with him, jostling its rider. Caroline's knee was pressed for a moment against Luis's booted ankle, and the colour flowered in her cheeks as he propelled the mare away.

'You ride like someone bent on a course to disaster,' he remarked dryly, just when she had been preparing herself for his approval. 'Do you always let your mount run away with you like that? Or were you simply incapable of doing anything about it?'

Caroline gave him an indignant look. 'I was in control,' she exclaimed defensively, patting the mare's neck with a knowledgeable hand. 'I'm sorry if our collision caused you some discomfort, but I wasn't aware your boots were so fragile!'

Luis's mouth drew down at the corners. 'In this terrain, one should always be in control,' he retorted grimly, directing her attention to a spot some four hundred yards away. 'Have you any idea how little time it takes for a herd of cattle to bear down on you, or the kind of injuries that can be sustained by so many plunging hooves?'

Caroline looked at the moving blur of darkness on the pale horizon. Until he pointed them out to her, she had been unaware of their presence, but now she quivered in the grip of her imagination. She had seen the frightening results of a stampede in films and on television, and she could certainly picture her terror if the herd turned this way. Even from her window they had seemed thick in number, and slightly menacing, and to be this near to them was itself unnerving.

'I—I didn't know, I didn't realise,' she said now, in futile expiation. 'What do we do now? Do we go back? I've never been this close to a herd of cattle before.'

'I doubt you have,' he conceded wryly, controlling the mettlesome gelding with the ease of long experience. 'And no, we do not go back. We ride through them. So long as we do not startle them, there is no danger.'

Caroline was not entirely convinced. The eyes she turned in Luis's direction then mirrored her indecision, and his stiffness eased as he attempted to reassure her.

'Come,' he said, urging his mount near to hers, and reaching out, he lifted the sombrero back on to her head. 'We will walk the horses for a while. That way, you can be sure we will disturb no one.'

The sun, which had previously been sheltering behind a bank of clouds, cleared then suddenly, and spread fingers of rose-pink and palest orange over the plain. Caroline could hear the birds squawking as they swooped overhead, and as she paced the mare beside the gelding, she had time to look about her and enjoy the increasing warmth upon her shoulders. She had tied the sleeves of her sweater around her shoulders, but she pulled it off now and fastened it to the front of her saddle. She rolled the sleeves of her shirt back to the elbows, exposing her slim arms to the sun, then felt slightly chastened when Luis looked her way. In his black pants and leather jerkin, he didn't seem bothered by the sun as she was, but he refrained from making any comment, and she determined not to let his attitude influence her.

'How far away is the sea?' she asked, shading her eyes, and endeavouring to ignore their approach to the herd, and Luis gave the matter some consideration.

'As the crow flies, some ten miles,' he replied briefly,

and Caroline gasped in surprise.

'So far?' she exclaimed, steering the mare round a clump of marsh grasses. 'But I thought—I mean—it seemed so near from the window of my room.'

'Distances can be deceptive,' remarked Luis carelessly, narrowing his eyes against the glare. 'Particularly when the ground is flat. Why?' He glanced sideways at her. 'Were you planning to dip your toes in the Gulf of Mexico?' He shook his head. 'I regret, you will have to save that doubtful privilege until Esteban chooses to take you in the Rover.'

Caroline sighed. 'I just thought it might have been nice to take Emilia to the beach,' she averred, avoiding his eyes. 'But if we have to go by road, I suppose I could take her myself. I can drive.'

Luis gave her a wry look. 'Do you really think Esteban will let you take Emilia out without his escort?' He shrugged. 'I think not.'

Caroline made an impatient gesture. 'Because I'm a woman alone? Oh, this is ridiculous!'

Luis made no response, and she expelled her breath with evident frustration. 'Do you mean to tell me that even in a car, we have to have a bodyguard?'

'If it pleases you to call it that, then yes.' Luis inclined his head. 'In any case, so far as Emilia is concerned there is always the danger of kidnapping, a common enough occurrence in these times. You would not wish to put her life in danger?'

Caroline pressed her lips together. 'No. No, of course not.'

'Good.' Luis made a dismissing gesture. 'So, you will do as Esteban says, *verdad*?'

Caroline moved her shoulders slightly resentfully, but she voiced no protest, as Luis took possession of the mare's bridle, to lead it through the grazing ranks of cattle.

Some of the beasts raised their heads to watch their progress, staring at them with wide brooding eyes, but as Luis had said, they were not aggressive. On the outer flanks of the herd they came upon several of the *gauchos*, whose job it was to guard the cattle, and they called greetings to Luis from their lazy bivouac beneath a clump of stunted cedars. They had lit a fire to make breakfast, and the scent of coffee was appetising, mingling with the inevitable smell of beans, and the thin corn pancakes, that were their staple diet. They offered to share their repast with the *patrón* and his lady, but although Caroline expected him to accept, Luis refused their generosity with formal politeness.

'I should not care for you to suffer some unfortunate stomach upset, because of my carelessness,' he told her flatly, as they put some distance between them and the drovers. 'The men are kind, but not always scrupulous, and you are not immune to infection.'

'You mean, if you had been alone, you would have accepted their invitation?' Caroline asked, glancing back over her shoulder, and Luis shrugged.

'Perhaps. It is of no matter.' He urged his horse forward. 'Come. We will ride for some way along the bank of the river, before we have to turn back.'

'Turn back?'

The consternation in Caroline's voice was unmistakable, but Luis only nodded. 'It is after seven, *señorita*,' he pointed out patiently, showing her the face of the slim gold watch on his wrist. 'And it will take us the better part of an hour to get back. You would not wish to be late for your lessons with Emilia, would you?'

Caroline supposed he was right, but she was disappointed that the time had passed so quickly, almost without her volition. She had wanted to talk to him, really talk to him, to get to know him better; and perhaps to discover for herself the real truth behind Esteban's assertions concerning Luis's mother. But now he was talking of turning back, and she had no idea when she might get another chance to be alone with him like this.

They cantered across a marshy expanse of ground, to where the somewhat muddy waters of the river surged forcefully downstream. Close at hand, she could see that the river had been swollen by the storms of two days before, and whereas from her window she had seen only the trees and shrubs that grew on the higher ground, now she saw the torn off branches of trees and other debris being swept irresistibly towards the ocean. Once the inflated carcase of some animal, trapped by the powerful undercurrent, swept by them, and Caroline shivered at the realisation of how little chance of survival anything would have, caught in that pitiless flow.

'My father drained this land,' remarked Luis, pulling the gelding's head round and compelling it along the bank. 'He deepened the channel of the river, and used the silt to raise the level of the ground. It greatly increased the value of his holding.'

'I can imagine.' Caroline urged the mare alongside him, looking down into the swirling waters. 'Have you lived here all your life, *señor*? Or did you, like your brother, go to university in England?'

Luis glanced her way broodingly, his brief spate of cordiality disappearing. 'I am sure the details of my education can be of no interest to you, *señorita*,' he essayed, without enthusiasm. 'Shall we ride to the ridge before turning back?'

'Your brother told me a little about your father, when he showed me round the house,' Caroline persisted, shifting in the saddle. 'We talked about your family. It was very interesting. He explained that you're really half-brothers, and that although you had the same father, you had different mothers——'

'*Basta!*' Luis's lean face darkened with sudden anger,

and he overrode her submission with grim determination. 'To what purpose do you tell me this, *señorita*?' he demanded. 'Of what possible interest could Esteban's confidences be to me?'

Caroline flushed. 'I was—simply making conversation, that's all,' she defended herself stiffly. 'You mentioned your father, and I—I reciprocated. I'm sorry, I didn't know the subject was taboo!'

Luis massaged the muscles at the back of his neck with an impatient hand, the action parting the lapels of his sleeveless jerkin, exposing the straining buttons of his dark shirt. 'It is not taboo, *señorita*,' he told her at last, expelling his breath with heavy emphasis. 'But do not take me for a fool either, whatever Esteban has said.'

Caroline was confused and embarrassed now, but somehow she had to remain composed. 'I don't know what you think your brother has said, *señor*,' she declared, taking the offensive. 'He spoke about the history of the house, and explained some of the legends associated with the area. And—and so far as your family is concerned, he—he merely defined the situation.'

'Indeed.' Luis's expression was sceptical now, his mouth oddly twisted, his attitude one of veiled contempt. 'You expect me to believe that? You did not then hope to provoke me into contradicting Esteban?'

'Contradicting him?' Caroline's face burned, in spite of herself. 'No, I——'

'Oh, let us have done with this,' Luis interrupted harshly. 'I know my brother, *señorita*. I know what he is capable of. I know what he must have told you. But I have no intention of satisfying your squalid curiosity by compounding his deficiency—do I make myself clear?' His lips curled. 'And if that is the real reason behind this sudden desire for horseback riding, then I regret, you have wasted your time!'

'You flatter yourself, *señor*.' Caroline caught her breath.

'I was looking forward to this outing. I was looking forward to getting away from the *hacienda*. Believe it or not, I have ridden before, and I've always enjoyed it. Accepting your company was just a means to an end, as it seems I am not allowed the freedom here I've been used to. I didn't ask for your brother's confidences, and I wouldn't presume to expect yours.' She drew another trembling breath and adjusted the strap of her sombrero before adding, unforgivably: 'But in one respect I would agree with Don Esteban. You are jealous of him. As jealous as hell! And that's why you're so damned touchy, when your brother's name is mentioned!'

It was a damning indictment, and although Caroline told herself it had been justified, she felt terribly guilty as she sat there, waiting for his denouncement.

But it never came. With an indifferent shrug of his shoulders, Luis dug his knees into the gelding's sides and the animal obediently broke into a canter. Within seconds, he was some distance ahead of her, widening the gap with every stride, and with a feeling of helpless compliance, Caroline was obliged to follow him.

The ridge he had mentioned was some half a mile away, a curving bluff of limestone, forming a natural ravine, at the bottom of which the river tumbled in contracted fury. Luis had reined his mount at the edge of the cliff, and Caroline rode up to him reluctantly, hanging some way back, aware that, so far as he was concerned at least, she had destroyed any hope of an amicable relationship between them.

When he turned his head to look at her, she had to steel herself not to glance away, then her heart lurched with sudden palpitation when she saw that he was smiling. He sat there, one arm resting lazily across the pommel of his saddle, his expression wry and slightly mocking, and she knew, without a shadow of a doubt, that no matter what Esteban said, jealousy was not the reason for Luis's behaviour.

'Feeling better?' he enquired, as she nudged her mare nearer to him, and Caroline made a gesture of defeat.

'I'm sorry,' she said, pushing back the hat and shaking her hair free. 'I was rude, and I'm sorry.' She looked at him ruefully. 'Will you forgive me?'

'There is nothing to forgive,' Luis retorted, straightening in the saddle. 'You have your opinions, and you are right to voice them. I am simply not used to such arbitrary candour.'

Caroline sighed. 'I shouldn't have said what I did,' she declared, shaking her head, then swung herself down from the saddle to walk tentatively to the rim of the ravine. 'Would you believe me if I said I didn't mean it?'

'I would advise you not to go too near the edge,' Luis commented dryly, and when she paid him no need, he too dismounted and, flexing his muscles, came to stand beside her.

Caroline was intensely aware of him, of the lean length of his thigh only inches from hers, and of the fact that she had only to stretch her fingers to touch him. But she was aware, too, of the precariousness of their relationship, and while she didn't want to do or say anything to disrupt it yet again, she had to relieve her own sense of inadequacy.

'Do you believe me?' she probed, looking up at him, and felt her breathing constrict when the intentness of his grey gaze locked with hers.

'What does it matter to you?' he asked, his voice taut with suppressed emotion. 'I shall be leaving here the day after tomorrow, *señorita*. My opinion is not important. It is with my brother you will have to deal.' He paused then, looking away from her to follow the plunging course of the river. 'But it may be that you are right,' he added, with some self-derision. 'Perhaps I am jealous of Esteban. Oh, yes—' this as she started to protest, 'perhaps I am. But not, I fear, for the reasons you imagine.'

'What do you mean?'

Caroline spoke huskily, but Luis had already turned away from her, adjusting the stirrup leathers hanging from his saddle, before thrusting his foot into the iron holster.

'Can you not guess?' he asked, settling himself more comfortably in the saddle, and her eyes widened as she gazed up at him. 'Never imagine a priest is not a man, *señorita*,' he concluded, causing her lips to part in confusion. 'Particularly, a priest who is not yet ordained.' He grimaced. 'In spite of my maternal heritage, I find that, ultimately, I am still my father's offspring.'

Caroline was bewildered. 'Your maternal heritage, *señor*? I—I don't understand——'

Luis bent his head, as if it was suddenly too heavy for his neck to support, and looked down at her in resignation. 'My mother lives at the Convent of the Sisters of the Annunciation, *señorita*. When my father died, she took refuge there, and it is my brother's wish that I should follow her example.'

CHAPTER FIVE

DON ESTEBAN had guests for dinner that evening.

They were a Señor and Señora Calveiro, from the neighbouring estate of Los Calvados, and their daughter, Josetta. Caroline, who had been informed of the invitation at lunch, had hoped to be allowed to take dinner alone in her room, but Don Esteban would not hear of it.

'Luis will be joining us, of course,' he said, spearing her with his dark gaze, and she wondered whether her unannounced outing with his brother had been reported to him. 'I shall expect you to make up the numbers, *señorita*, and I am sure the Calveiros will wish to compliment me on my good fortune.'

'You're very kind, *señor*.'

Caroline had answered politely enough, but inside, she had dreaded the evening ahead, and the inevitable association with his brother. After that disturbing exchange on the ridge, they had ridden back to the house without any further opportunity for conversation, and once there, Luis had speedily excused himself from her presence. She had suspected he was already regretting his earlier frankness, and she doubted he would welcome an evening spent in the company of a confessor. She had been responsible, of course, it was all her fault, and her own feelings were so confused, the last thing she wanted was to make the situation any harder—for either of them.

But she had had little time to reflect on these thoughts. The advent of the maid with her breakfast tray had interrupted the hasty shower she was taking, and afterwards, dressed neatly in a navy shirt and brace skirt, she had found Emilia already in the library, awaiting her.

The little girl had evidently decided the easier course was to obey her father, and Caroline was glad she had had the foresight to prepare the next day's lesson the previous morning, while Emilia was writing an essay. In future, she would have to find time to prepare their lessons on a more regulated basis, devoting different days to different subjects, but for the present, she concentrated on keeping the child busy, and interested. Mexican history had never been Caroline's strong point, but now she found herself reading about the Spanish conquest, the subsequent religious conversion, and ultimately, the mingling of Spanish and Indian blood to produce the *mestizo* race that presently predominated. She studied the campaigns of Benito Juarez and Porfirio Diaz, the latter dictatorship primarily responsible for the flourishing wealth of the *hacenderos*, and the revolution of 1910 which made such a hero of Pancho Villa, and realised how limited her knowledge had been up to that time. The more she learned, however, the more it fascinated her, and she refused to acknowledge that she was in any way influenced by her involuntary involvement with Luis.

Lunch was again a buffet meal, and for once Caroline was glad of Doña Isabel's presence to divert Esteban's attention from herself. Nevertheless, the dark-eyed patron of San Luis found plenty of occasions to bring her into the conversation, and she was made increasingly aware that little went on that he did not know about.

And yet, although there were several occasions when she had an opportunity to tell him that she had been riding with his brother, somehow she never seemed to find the right words. It didn't occur to her that Luis might have told him. Instinctively she guessed that he would leave it to her to make that decision, but the idea of telling Esteban, of laying herself open to his mockery and possible contempt, promoted only constraint, and she escaped after the meal feeling distinctly cowardly.

As on the previous afternoon, she sought the refuge of her own room, and fell asleep on her bed. She had intended to prepare the following day's lessons for Emilia, and write to her mother, but exhaustion overtook her, and she knew nothing more until the sun was rapidly sinking into the west.

She got off the bed reluctantly, aware of the approaching dinner party, and spent several minutes gazing at her reflection with critical eyes. The rest had left a slumbrous languor about her, and there were faintly bruised shadows on her eyelids. She had slept too soundly, she decided, refusing to acknowledge their significance, and dismissed the uneasy realisation that the last thing she had thought of was Luis's face, when he told her he was his father's son. Unbidden, Doña Isabel's words came back to her, the old lady's angry denunciation of the woman she had seen in the *hacienda*. All of a sudden, it did not seem so incredible that there was some female in Luis's life, and Caroline perceived her own reactions to it with a sense of impatience.

Leaving the bedroom, she stripped off her clothes and took a cold shower, revelling in the brisk spray, dispersing the lingering threads of lassitude. It would not do to face her employer without being fully alert, she reflected dryly, and while she might resent his arbitrary use of her presence, he was her employer, and she felt obliged to accommodate him.

She took the only black dress she possessed out of the wardrobe and flung it on the bed, studying its simple lines without enthusiasm. It was made of a synthetic fibre, that combined the uncrushability of polyester with the softness of silk, and she had bought it to attend a cocktail party with Andrew, and the memories it evoked were not welcome.

It had been one of those professorial gatherings, beloved of the lecturing fraternity, and just after Caroline had taken her final exams. Tricia was ill again, some complication after another of her nervous upsets, and Andrew had cast caution to the winds and invited Caroline to join him. There had been some eyebrows raised at the sight of the handsome young professor escorting his erstwhile student, Caroline remembered ruefully, fingering the soft black folds. In spite of her father's position, their relationship was untenable. He was a married man, and when Caroline encountered Tricia on the campus the following week, her understanding had left Caroline feeling like a bitch. It was then she had begun to see the futility of her love for Andrew. He was never going to divorce Tricia. Her father, the dean, would see to that. And because Caroline's own father was also involved, there seemed only one alternative.

With a sigh, Caroline slipped the dress over her head,

and acknowledged without conceit that its darkness complemented her extreme fairness. Against the sombre
fabric, her hair had the sheen of silver, and the sun had
only tinted the pale contours of her face. The halter neckline exposed most of her neck and shoulders, and the
downy hollow of her back, but she couldn't help it. It was
the most suitable thing she possessed, and she had seen
many more provocative garments at the hotel in Merida.

Dinner was at eight, but Don Esteban had asked her to
join him for a pre-dinner aperitif at seven-thirty. It was a
little after that time when Caroline left her room, and she
was walking with her usual haste along the gloomy corridor when a door to her right suddenly opened. She was
so shocked, she faltered in her stride, for she had supposed
herself the only occupant of this wing. But Luis's unexpected appearance disabused her of that belief, and she
gazed at him speechlessly for a few moments, before recovering her equilibrium.

'I am sorry. Did I startle you?' he asked, emerging
from the room and closing the door, and she expelled her
breath with feeling.

He was formally dressed this evening, in a wine-
coloured velvet evening suit, the matching silk of his shirt
enhanced by a froth of lace. On many men, she realised,
the extravagance would have looked feminine, but with
Luis's hard features, no such comparison was necessary.
The shoulders beneath the soft pile of his jacket were
broad and unpadded, the thighs mounding the material
like a second skin were powerful and muscular, and she
knew from experience that his sinewy strength had all the
resourcefulness of a predator.

'I didn't—I didn't know your rooms were on this
corridor,' she admitted, as he fell into step beside her.
'It—it always seems so empty.'

'They are not,' Luis disillusioned her politely. 'I have
been visiting Tia Isabel, that is all. It is she, and not I,

who shares this wing with you.'

'Oh!' Caroline was aware of a sudden empty feeling, not wholly due to a sense of disappointment. Of all the occupants of the *hacienda*, Doña Isabel was the last person she would have chosen to share her seclusion, and a feathering of goosebumps rippled her flesh.

'She is harmless, you know,' Luis remarked quietly, as if aware of her apprehension, and Caroline glanced quickly at him. His perception where she was concerned was quite remarkable, but in this instance his reassurance was not convincing.

'When she is lucid,' she retorted, as they reached the head of the stairs, and preceded him down them before he could make any further comment.

Don Esteban's guests had arrived, and were talking with him in the main *salón*, an imposing room, with many fine pictures, and furniture from the period of the last emperor. But it was not the room that held Caroline's attention this evening, but the four men and women who awaited her there, and her mouth went dry when she encountered their critical gaze.

She had been right to wear black, she acknowledged flatly, but that was her only merit. The gowns of the two women who stood with Don Esteban bore no resemblance to hers, and their hostility was evident in every word and gesture. From the protection afforded by severely-collared dresses, with long buttoned sleeves, they looked down their thin noses at the outrageous English girl, subjecting her to their censure, and unveiled disapproval.

To Caroline's dismay, Luis seemed amused by this display of self-righteousness, and it was left to Don Esteban to rescue the situation. Unlike his guests, he obviously found Caroline's appearance stunning, and he came towards her purposefully and possessed himself of her hand.

'You look—*bellisima, senorita*,' he informed her gallantly, raising her fingers to his lips. Then he glanced round at the Calveiros, and made a bow. 'What a fortunate man I am to have three such beautiful women at my table!'

The introductions were brief, to Caroline's relief, and soon over, and then Josetta Calveiro deserted her parents to move to Luis's side. Caroline heard her chattering away to him eagerly in their own language, as she was appropriated by Don Esteban, and felt an unwelcome sense of resentment. It was obvious that Josetta was very young, and probably very immature, but did Luis have to behave as if he found her conversation absorbing?

'You are a stranger to Mexico, *señorita*,' Señora Calveiro addressed her now, and Caroline endeavoured to concentrate on what she was saying.

'Oh, yes. Yes.' She forced a faint smile. 'I've never crossed the Atlantic before. It's an entirely new experience for me.'

'And for Emilia, too, I am sure,' endorsed Señora Calveiro, through tight lips. 'It must be quite enlightening for the child to be taught by someone who is obviously so—independent, Esteban. Beware she does not learn all the wrong things.'

Esteban's thick lips parted, as he selected another glass from the tray, proffered by a hovering waiter. 'Miss Leyton understands our situation here, Doña Julia,' he affirmed, swallowing the lime-flavoured cocktail without grace or hesitation, and taking another. 'Besides, it is good for Emilia to learn of the world outside San Luis.' His fingers touched Caroline's in mute approval. 'Who knows, we may all benefit from this young lady's arrival.'

Señor Calveiro chose to intercede at that point, taking his host away to discuss some aspect of cattle-raising, and Caroline was left to combat Señora Calveiro's animosity alone.

'You have made an ally of your employer, I perceive,' the soberly-garbed *matrona* remarked coldly. 'But have a care, *señorita*. Don Esteban has been the aspiration of many a hopeful intrigue, but to my knowledge he has never sought to repeat the mistakes of the past.'

Caroline's fingers tightened on her glass, as the woman's meaning became evident. 'I can assure you, *señora*, I have no such aspirations,' she responded politely. 'My reasons for being here are precisely what they seem. I was employed, at the instigation of Don Esteban, by Señora Garcia, and if he finds my work satisfactory then my purpose has been achieved.'

Señora Calveiro frowned, regarding her daughter's continuing conversation with Luis with as little enthusiasm as Caroline. 'I did not know that Juana's mother had any part in this,' she murmured, almost absently. And then, returning her attention to the girl at her side, she added: 'I am surprised Esteban permitted it.'

'As Emilia's grandmother, surely Señora Garcia is entitled to the privilege,' suggested Caroline awkwardly, not quite knowing how to answer her, and Señora Calveiro's eyes wandered again.

'Perhaps,' she murmured thoughtfully, tasting her cocktail as if it was bitter, 'but after the scandalous way Juana treated Esteban, it is a measure of his tolerance that he permits any contact.' She shrugged, arching her thin brows in an expression of inconsequence. 'So long as the child is happy, I suppose we must all make allowances.'

Caroline nodded, wishing desperately that someone would make allowances for her. With Esteban ensconced in conversation at the other side of the room, and Josetta monopolising Luis, she was obliged to humour the elderly *dueña*, and it was becoming something of a strain.

Then she turned, and found Luis's eyes upon her.

Until that instant she had not thought he was aware of her. Their conversation upstairs had given her no cause to think otherwise; he had not even complimented her on her appearance. But in that unguarded moment, when she intercepted his brooding gaze, she knew she had been mistaken, and she also knew that his interest in Josetta's chatter was no greater than hers in Señora Calveiro's.

Responding to the silent appeal in her eyes, Luis excused himself from the Mexican girl and crossed the richly-woven pile of the carpet. His booted feet made little sound on the fabric, and the lithe resolution of his movements reminded Caroline of a feline. There was something intensely sensual in imagining the muscled hardness of his body beneath the yielding texture of his clothes, like the supple power of a jaguar, beneath the deceptive softness of its skin.

'Señora,' he greeted Josetta's mother smoothly, returning his empty glass to the tray, without taking another. 'I trust Miss Leyton's presence has assured you that Emilia is in good hands.'

'Miss Leyton has been telling me that Doña Elena made the arrangements,' Señora Calveiro declared stiffly. 'Without Esteban's good nature, where would we all be?'

'Where indeed?' murmured Luis politely, his thigh brushing Caroline's as he moved from one foot to the other. 'Esteban should be an example to us all.'

Caroline glanced at him swiftly as he spoke, expecting to see the mockery in his face, but he looked perfectly serious, and Señora Calveiro endorsed his trite statement. 'I am pleased to hear you appreciate this, Luis,' she said, with less hostility than before. 'I know your mother would agree with me when I say that you owe Esteban a lot, and not every brother is willing to forgive and forget.'

'How succinctly you put it, *señora*,' observed Luis, with a smile that Caroline watched with blank disbelief. 'I will give your good wishes to my mother, the next time I see her, and you can be assured she will be interested to hear of your approval.'

Surprisingly, this did not seem to meet with such a

favourable reaction, and it was perhaps fortunate that a waiter appeared at that moment to announce that dinner was served. Señora Calveiro immediately moved to join her husband and Esteban, and as Josetta was likewise engaged, for a few unguarded moments Caroline and Luis were alone.

'I would thank you for rescuing me, if I knew what you were doing,' she breathed, bending to deposit her half empty glass on the low marble-topped table behind her. 'I'm sorry, I didn't realise you were such an ardent sympathiser of your brother's. If I've said or done anything to offend you, please accept my apologies.'

'Do not be foolish,' Luis exhorted her roughly, his lean fingers curving round her wrist, under cover of their bodies. 'Would you have had me start an argument with her, and arouse her sour suspicions? So far as Doña Julia is concerned, I am—how do you call it?—the black sheep, *no*, and nothing I can say or do will alter her opinion.'

'But why?' Caroline gazed at him, intensely aware of those strong fingers gripping her arm, and his lips compressed impatiently, bracketing his mouth with harsh lines.

'Did not Esteban apprise you of the facts of Emilia's conception?' he demanded grimly. 'Did he not divulge his heartache at his wife's indiscretions?'

'No!' Caroline moved her head negatively, and almost involuntarily his hand slid down to hers. She doubted he was as aware of their unknowing intimacy as she was, but when his fingers probed between hers, they parted to receive him.

'He will,' said Luis now, his dark face taut with emotion, and Caroline's senses spun.

'You mean—Emilia is your daughter?' she whispered, dreading his confirmation, then caught her breath when his face convulsed.

'No!' he denied savagely, jerking her towards him, so that for a pain-sweet moment she was close to his hard body. 'Juana and I were never lovers. Emilia is not my daughter. Though why I should feel the need to defend myself to you, I do not know.'

'No.'

Caroline's response was choked but faint, and he looked down at her almost resentfully, his eyes smouldering with passion. 'Oh, yes,' he contradicted her at last, his mouth suddenly sensual. 'Yes, I know. But there is nothing—*nothing*—I can do about it.'

'And what is it you can do nothing about, *mi hermano*?' rasped another voice near Caroline's ear, and they moved apart almost guiltily, Caroline thrusting her suddenly trembling hands behind her back. Esteban had come to join them, moving silently as his brother had done, and Caroline wondered agonisingly how long he had been standing there, listening.

'I was merely confirming Señora Calveiro's opinion of you, Esteban,' Luis assured him flatly, causing his brother's colour to rise with unbecoming haste. 'She is such a—how shall I put it?—an admirer of yours, and I was confessing to Miss Leyton how—humble you make us all feel.'

Esteban's mouth compressed. 'You are not amusing, Luis,' he countered coldly. 'And Miss Leyton should know better than to listen to you.' His hand reached purposefully for Caroline's elbow. 'Come, *señorita*. You will sit with me during dinner, so that Señora Calveiro shall not think you take my brother's vows lightly.'

Caroline's colour rivalled his as they entered the dining room. She was aware of the Calveiros' eyes upon her, and of the almost brutal strength underlying the soft fingers gripping her arm—and most of all, she was aware of Luis's presence behind them, and the disturbing connotations behind Don Esteban's warning.

It was not an easy meal. Although she tried to concentrate on the food, Caroline's eyes were irresistibly drawn to the foot of the table, where Luis was making conversation again with Josetta. What had he meant by the things he had said? What interpretation could she put upon his actions? And why should she feel so affected by it, when she knew of the circumstances of his background?

'You find my brother's company appealing?' enquired her host, under cover of the servants removing her scarcely-touched plate of soup, and Caroline's wandering thoughts were speared.

'I beg your pardon?' she queried, playing for time, shocked out of her reverie, and unable to marshall her defences, and Esteban's lips curved.

'My brother,' he repeated, in a low voice, helping her to a generous portion of sliced chicken, served with rice and peppers, and a rich, strongly-smelling sauce, and Caroline's stomach revolted. 'Don Luis. His attentions flatter you, perhaps?'

Caroline moistened her dry lips. 'He—I—I find his company—pleasant, yes,' she conceded rather unevenly. 'And please—no more.' She held up unsteady fingers to the waiter. 'I—I'm not very hungry.'

'No?' Esteban looked sideways at her. 'And why is that, *señorita*? Do you not find our menus tasty? Or has my brother robbed you of what appetite you had?'

Caroline took a deep breath. 'Don Esteban, your—your brother has said nothing to rob me of my appetite. I simply don't eat a lot, that's all.' She determinedly dipped her fork into the rice on her plate and took a mouthful. 'This is very nice. I—I like it.'

Don Esteban shrugged his broad shoulders and applied himself to his food for a while, but just when Caroline was beginning to breathe more easily, he turned to her again.

'You may think I interfere,' he said, causing her to look up at him with wide, startled eyes. 'But I know my brother better than you do, and it concerns me that you might—misinterpret his—actions.'

Caroline expelled her breath unevenly. 'Honestly, *señor*——'

'No, I insist you listen to me, *señorita*.' He frowned, concentrating for a moment on the food on his plate. Then he looked at her again. 'I have told you, have I not, of our relationship?' And when Caroline permitted an uneasy nod, he continued: 'What I have not told you, *señorita*, is that there is another reason why my brother and I can never be friends——'

'*Señor*——'

'—He destroyed my marriage, *señorita*.'

Caroline put down her fork, and clasped her hands tightly together in her lap. She should have expected this, of course. After what Señora Calveiro had said, she should have known what was to come. What she could not accept was why Don Esteban should wish her to know this.

'I have shocked you,' he said now, refilling his wine glass. 'I am sorry.' He swallowed some of the transparent liquid. 'But you are young, *señorita*, and vulnerable, and I should not like you to be—hurt.'

Caroline drew a deep breath. 'Why are you telling me this, *señor*? Lu—Don Luis—and I scarcely know one another. And—and as you pointed out, he will be returning to the seminary soon.'

Esteban inclined his head. 'Yet it comes to my notice that you have spent much time in his company during these last few days. Did you not go riding with him this morning? Or was it his village woman who accompanied him?'

Caroline's face flamed. 'You must know it was me,' she replied stiffly. 'But—but it was at my instigation. I—I wanted to see outside the gates of the *hacienda*. Don Luis offered to accompany me.'

'I see.' Esteban studied the wine in his glass. 'You did not think to ask me if you could ride beyond the gates of the *hacienda*?'

Caroline sighed. 'I did think of it, yes——'

'—but Luis was there, hmm?'

'You were otherwise engaged, *señor*. Besides, I—well, Don Luis told me you didn't ride.'

'Ah!' Esteban swirled the wine around in its crystal container. 'Luis told you that, did he?'

'Isn't it true?'

Caroline's question stemmed as much from a desire to reassure herself that she had not been mistaken about Luis than from any real interest in Esteban's abilities. And as if aware of this, her host regarded her with mocking eyes.

'Let us say that like all the things my brother will tell you, there is a grain of truth behind it, *señorita*,' he replied. He bent his head. 'But we have talked of Luis long enough. Come, tell me about Emilia. Has her education been neglected? Can you assure me that it is not beyond repair?'

This was easier ground, and in discussing his daughter's education Caroline found an almost painful relief. Despite the nuances overlying his comments concerning her predecessor, she was able to talk with confidence about Emilia's intelligence, and he was reluctantly impressed by the child's evident aptitude for study.

'So you think Emilia has the makings of a scholar?' he remarked at last, draining his glass once again. 'What a pity she is not one of your English misses, *señorita*. Who knows, maybe she, too, might have wished to assert her independence.'

Caroline forced a faint smile, but she was aware that Don Esteban was drinking far more than anyone else at the table, and what was even more disturbing, Señora Calveiro, and her daughter, were watching them closely, as if she was to blame for his studied neglect of his other guests.

The meal dragged to its inevitable conclusion, and Caroline was heartily relieved when Don Esteban acknowledged the servant's intimation that coffee had been prepared in the *salón*.

'Let me help you,' he said, getting to his feet to draw back her chair, and she saw that despite the amount of wine he had consumed throughout the meal, he was still perfectly capable of supporting himself. It was she who stumbled as she rose, her haste to get away from the table overriding her attempt at composure, and Don Esteban's fingers slid about her waist, as he rescued her temporary loss of balance.

'No hurry, *señorita*,' he murmured, his wine-scented breath fanning her cheek, and a sense of revulsion out of all proportion to the incident brought a wave of heat over her body.

'Thank you, I can manage,' she got out unevenly, drawing herself away from him, but not before she had seen the Calveiros exchange a significant glance that mirrored all too clearly their opinion of her behaviour. What did they think she was? she wondered impotently, marching ahead of Don Esteban, flags of colour burning in her cheeks. Were they so out of touch with everyday living that they imagined her only reason for coming here was to find a husband? Did they seriously believe she was interested in Don Esteban? Was it beyond the realms of the Calveiros' experience that a woman should want more from life than the security of a husband?

In the *salón*, she sought the isolation of a satin-covered-armchair, withdrawing herself mentally, if not physically, from the company. She accepted the cup of coffee proffered by an olive-skinned maid with trembling fingers, then reviewed her position, in the light of the present situation.

It seemed obvious she had made a mistake in coming here. Aside from the remoteness of the *hacienda*, she was being reluctantly drawn into the personal lives of her employers. It was useless to tell herself that it wasn't important, that she had a job to do, and she should do it. She was involved, unwillingly or otherwise, and what was more, her motives were being tried and judged by people who knew nothing about her, who lived in a society confined by its own limitations.

'You seem—troubled,' remarked a quiet voice beside her, and she looked up tensely into Luis's lean dark face.

'I am,' she said, in no mood to fence words with him. 'I think I should not have come here.'

Luis squatted down easily beside her, the soft material of his pants taut over the muscles of his thighs. 'And what reason do you have for coming to this conclusion?' he enquired flatly. 'Do not distress yourself on my account. I shall be leaving soon. You have nothing to fear from me.'

Caroline caught her breath. 'It—I—it has nothing to do with you,' she exclaimed huskily. 'I—I just feel a man would be more—suitable in this post.'

Luis sighed. 'So—what did Esteban say to you?'

'Don Esteban?' Caroline's tongue circled her lips. 'Why, nothing.'

Luis frowned. 'So you had come to this decision before you came down to dinner?'

Caroline hesitated. 'Not exactly.'

'Then——'

'Oh, if you must know, I feel—I feel as if Señora Calveiro thinks I have—designs on your brother.' She bent her head. 'And I'm not sure he doesn't think that too.'

Luis shrugged, the grey eyes, almost on a level with hers, narrowed and speculative. 'And why did you come, *señorita*?'

Caroline gasped. 'You know why! Because I needed a job. Because it sounded—it sounded——'

'—exciting?'

'No. *Interesting!*' Caroline became aware that once again Señora Calveiro was watching her. 'Believe it or not, but I am not looking for a husband.'

'You have a lover in England?' he asked in a low voice, and her cheeks flamed once again. He had no right to ask her such a question, and she was tempted to tell him so. But then it occurred to her that perhaps this was a means of defence, and straightening her spine, she said levelly: 'There is someone—yes,' and had the satisfaction of knowing that for once she had disconcerted him.

Then, with a brief shrug of his shoulders, Luis got to his feet again. 'I would say he is a foolish man, *señorita,*' he remarked, winning the point after all, and pushing his hands into the pockets of his jacket, he gave her a polite nod before walking silently away.

To Caroline's relief, the party broke up soon after. In spite of her fears, Don Esteban remained sober enough to wish farewell to his guests, and she made her escape in the melée, only desiring the peace and seclusion of her room. The shadowy corridor had never seemed longer, with the knowledge of Doña Isabel's presence behind one of the closed doors, but she reached her room without mishap and leant back wearily against the panels.

What a tangled web her thoughts had created, darting and weaving among the jumbled threads of their relationships. If only Esteban's wife had still been alive; if only Luis had been her employer; and yet did not the two things contradict themselves? If Luis had been her employer, she would not have wished for him to have a wife. She hardly knew what she wished any more. She was tired. It had been a long day. And even if she only stayed for the probationary month, there was still more than three weeks to go . . .

CHAPTER SIX

IN the morning, things looked different.

Caroline had slept shallowly, and she awakened early, spending several minutes on her balcony, watching the sun's rays colour the sky. It was another beautiful morning, the air cool and refreshing, the distant shimmer of the ocean like a mirage on the horizon. The heady scents from the garden below her windows filled her room with their perfume, and although she knew that later the heat would make their petals droop, now they blossomed voluptuously, spreading their velvety stamens and reaching greedily for the sun.

She rested her elbows on the balcony rail and cupped her chin in her hands. This was her fourth day at the *hacienda*, she thought pensively. Was she going to give it up so easily? Was she really going to admit defeat, and return to her home in England?

She sighed, aware of her uncertainty now that the sun was shining again. Had she not perhaps overreacted to circumstances that were new to her? Was she over-sensitive to other people's criticism? After all, she was not like them, and their restrictions should not be allowed to interfere with her determination. She was letting their attitudes influence her decision, and that had to be foolish.

Señora Calveiro was to blame. It was she, as much as anyone, who had put the doubt in Caroline's mind. Intimating that she might be interested in Don Esteban, insinuating a relationship that was wholly imaginary. No doubt, she had her own daughter's future in mind, and it was true that Don Esteban might present an eligible image in her mind—a widower, with only one child, not too old, and undoubtedly wealthy. If Josetta appeared to prefer his brother to Don Esteban, that also was not important, for wasn't it already decided that Don Luis should follow his mother's example?

Caroline's teeth dug into her lower lip, unable to deny any longer the apprehension she felt when she thought of Luis's departure. It was ridiculous, she knew, but somehow she felt *safer* with him around. Yet that in itself was crazy. What had she possibly to be afraid of here? Don Esteban might drink too much, but he was a civilised human being, not some perverted monster, who threatened her virginity. Emilia was just a child, and Doña Isabel, for all her eccentricities, was frail and elderly. She was more than a match for any of them, she told herself, and shutting all thoughts of Luis from her mind, she went to take her shower.

Half an hour later, in a white camisole top and black and white patterned skirt, she left her room and walked quickly along the corridor and down the stairs. It was too early for the maid to bring her breakfast, and she had decided to take a walk outside before the heat became too oppressive.

She opened the door into the ante-room that she and Luis had used the previous morning, then tried the door that led outside. It was locked. There was no key to turn to give her her freedom, and no matter how she tried, the heavy wood would not budge.

Frustration brought a beading of sweat to her forehead. Damn, she thought, damn, damn, damn, and knew the panicky feeling of a prisoner, confronted by the irrevocable boundaries of his cell. Not that the *hacienda* bore any resemblance to a prison, she thought, struggling against hysteria, but its cloying atmosphere was suddenly stifling.

Turning away, she clutched at the handle of the door

that bore the crucifix nailed to its surface. The iron latch
lifted easily, and she drew back to allow the studded
wood its outward passage, peering half apprehensively
into the shadowy interior beyond the door.

A flight of stone steps led down and, licking her lips,
Caroline ventured forward. It was cool in the draught
wafting up from below, and she wondered rather anxiously whether there were dungeons below the *hacienda*.
Had the Spanish built dungeons below their palaces? She
thought somehow they had, and while this was not a
palace, it was very old.

But the light grew a little stronger as she reached the
bottom of the steps, and what she had thought was another door turned out to be heavy velvet curtains concealing the chamber that now confronted her. It was a
chapel, a small but exquisitely decorated chapel, with a
damask-covered altar, lit by candles. The screen behind
the altar was intricately carved, and there were statues of
the Virgin and Child, and another of the patron saint of
San Luis de Merced. The statues were gowned in richly
textured robes, glittering with precious stones, and the
altar-cloth and the velvet kneeling hassocks were brilliant
splashes of colour within the chapel's grey walls. It was so
vivid, and so unexpected, that she caught her breath, and
the man who had been kneeling almost out of sight
behind one of the stone pillars that supported the roof of
the chapel turned to gaze half angrily at her.

It was Luis, unfamiliar in a long black cassock, his
expression mirroring his impatience with her for having
interrupted his devotions, and Caroline's feet took her
backward, seeking the soundless anonymity behind the
curtains.

'*Wait!*'

His harsh admonition arrested her, and she faltered,
watching his forceful approach with uncertain eyes.
Seeing him like this was unnerving somehow, a confirma-

tion of what hitherto had seemed scarcely credible, and
her own emotions clawed inside her, making a mockery of
the frozen face she turned towards him.

'I'm sorry,' she said, as he neared her. 'I didn't know, I
didn't think——' She broke off as he halted in front of
her, and then added awkwardly: 'The door into the
garden was locked. I couldn't find the key.'

Luis studied her anxious face with a dark intensity,
then made an indifferent gesture. 'It is no secret that I
come here,' he said, gesturing round at the altar. 'It is the
only place in my father's house where I feel truly at
peace.' She noticed he did not say his *brother*'s house. 'But
you wanted to go outside. I will show you the way.'

'Oh, please . . .' Caroline put out a hand. 'Do—do go
on with—with whatever you were doing. I mean—don't
let me disturb you——'

Luis looked down at her imploring fingers, then
bent to haul the long black robe up and over his head.
Beneath, he was wearing a black shirt and corded pants,
and he thrust the enveloping tunic aside and ran smoothing fingers over his hair.

'Come,' he said, starting through the curtains, and
with a curiously dry mouth she followed him up the steps
and into the ante-room.

The outer door was still immovable, and bidding her
wait for him, Luis disappeared into the main body of the
house. He returned a few moments later, weighing a
handful of keys between his fingers, and after a moment's
examination he found the one which opened the door.

'My brother becomes more security-conscious as he
grows older,' he remarked, turning the key. 'This door
was never locked in my memory.'

Caroline recalled what Doña Isabel had said about the
use of the *puerta accesoria*, and coloured. Perhaps Don
Esteban had had the door locked to prevent the woman
his aunt had seen from entering the *hacienda*? The woman

they both believed was Luis's mistress!

'Is something wrong?' Luis had observed her sudden stillness and Caroline forced herself to move past him, out of the door and into the sun-drenched morning air.

'Why, no. What could be wrong?' she responded tautly, turning her face up to the sunlight, and then was disconcerted still further when he fell into step beside her.

'Tell me,' he said, 'why do you think the door was locked? To keep you in?' He paused. 'Or to keep someone else out?'

Caroline's tongue appeared briefly. 'As—as you said, *señor*, your—your brother is aware of the value of his possessions——'

Luis snorted. 'But you do not believe this?'

Caroline bent to touch the petals of a scarlet hibiscus, growing with others in wild profusion beside the zigzag paving of the path. She was glad of the diversion to hide her expression from him, and choosing not to answer him, she inhaled their delicate fragrance. 'Do you know,' she said, brushing pollen from her fingers, 'people pay a lot of money for plants like these back in England? We have to keep them indoors, and cultivate them so carefully, whereas here they grow like weeds.'

She heard his angry intake of breath, and the impatient oath that slipped unbidden from his lips, but she did not turn, and he strode past her, leading the way down shallow terraced steps to a trellised rose garden. She hesitated for a moment, but then, shading her eyes against the glare, she followed him, treading the path that wound between sculpted banks of foliage. There were bees buzzing among the flowers, and butterflies rose in startled flight as her shadow crossed their path, and the natural barriers of nature closed around them like the walls of a maze.

The path gave out beside a lily pond, where exotically coloured fish darted among the trailing blossoms. Occa-

sionally they came to the surface, to feed from the suici-
dally-reckless insects that skimmed the still water, and the
rippling sound they made reminded Caroline that it must
be almost time for breakfast. But when she turned, Luis
was standing right behind her, blocking her path, and she
was obliged to walk round the pond to put some space
between them.

'I leave tomorrow morning,' he said at last, when Caroline, who had been searching her thoughts desperately
for something to say, was almost at the end of her tether,
and his words fell like chips of ice between them. 'This
may be the last time we meet. Tonight I have to attend a
wedding in the village, and tomorrow I shall be gone
before you awake.'

'I—I see.' Caroline swallowed hard. 'I—I—we shall
miss you.'

'*We?*'

'Emilia and I,' she declared defensively, and he inclined his head in silent acquiescence. Then: 'Will—will
you be away long?'

'You mean—will I be coming back?' he amended
harshly, pacing slowly round the circuit of the pool. 'Not
for some time, I think.'

'Oh!'

Caroline was shocked at her own reactions to this.
Even after what had happened this morning, even after
seeing him in the robes of the priesthood, she could not
reconcile herself to his calling. He was a man, and he
disturbed her as no other man ever had, not even
Andrew, she acknowledged unwillingly, and the emptiness his going evoked inside her was a physical thing.

'I—I'm sorry,' she said now, as he reached her, and
stopped to lift one booted foot and place it on the raised
balustrade that surrounded the pool. 'I—I know
Emilia——'

She broke off abruptly, unable to go on beneath the

level scrutiny of those dark-lashed grey eyes. She could not continue mouthing platitudes, when she was so overwhelmingly conscious of the hard strength of his body only inches away from her own, and her complicity filled her with shame.

'Will you stay?' he asked now, turning his head to look at her, and she endeavoured to present a calm façade.

'Stay?' she echoed, her mind blank for a moment. 'Oh—oh, you mean here, at San Luis. I—I honestly don't know.' She moved her shoulders helplessly. 'It—depends.'

'On what?'

He was persistent, and expelling her breath unsteadily, she made a helpless gesture. 'Whether—whether my—my work is satisfactory, whether your brother is happy with Emilia's progress, whether I—I find the work rewarding——'

'And that is all?'

She bent her head, the silky strands of pale hair falling about her ears. 'I suppose you're referring to what I said last night,' she ventured. 'About—about Señora Calveiro.'

'She had appeared to upset you. Or was that Estaban?'

Caroline shook her head. 'I was tired last night. I may have been a little—hasty.'

'So you will stay?'

'I don't know, do I?' She lifted her head, and her eyes, wide and indignant, met the naked passion in his.

'You must go,' he said, with sudden violence. 'I do not want you here. Go home. Go back to England. Go back to this man, who cares for you in a way I cannot understand.'

Caroline's breathing quickened. 'What do you mean?' she whispered, gazing at him tremulously. 'What has my staying to do with you?'

Luis's mouth hardened. 'I should say nothing, of

course, should I not?' he retorted. 'You are here at my brother's instigation. You are his employee. And if you were a little reckless in accepting a situation so far from the people and places you are used to, that also should not be my concern.' He made a savage gesture. 'But it is! It had been so ever since I saw you in the hotel in Las Estadas, and although I tell myself I should care nothing, that you are old enough to make your own decision, you are a constant cause of vexation to me!'

'I'm sorry.' Caroline was taken aback. She had not realised he might feel *concern* for her. 'I assure you, I'm perfectly capable of taking care of myself.'

'Are you? *Are you?*'

Without another word he put out his hand, his fingers curving behind her nape, under the silky sway of her hair. Although she would have drawn back, his grip was purposeful, compelling her irrevocably towards him, drawing her against the upraised curve of his leg. Her hands, balled against his chest, were no defence to his strength and determination, and he bent his head without effort and covered her mouth with his.

His kiss was light and soon over, his lips barely brushing hers, and stiff, as if he held himself in check. 'You see!' he said, and he was unable to conceal the raw emotion in his voice. 'You are as helpless as a baby in the hands of a strong man, and you must realise my brother is no celibate!'

Caroline quivered in his grasp. 'As you are.'

'As I am,' he conceded harshly.

Caroline moistened her lips. 'A—aside from the woman—the woman who comes from the village,' she choked impulsively, and the darkening anger of his expression was evidence enough of his comprehension.

'So. You have learned a lot in a very short time, *señorita*,' he grated, releasing her abruptly, and removing his foot from the balustrade. 'And already you are prepared to think the worst.'

'I didn't say that.' Caroline's legs felt like jelly, but she had to go on. 'Is—isn't it true? Is there no woman?'

Luis hunched his shoulders. 'Oh, yes,' he said, and his response caused a pain like a knife to twist in Caroline's stomach. 'Oh, yes, there is a woman. Her name is Ana Pascale.' His lips twisted as he turned to look contemptuously at her. 'And what do you think we do together, when she confesses her sins to me?'

Caroline moved her head helplessly from side to side. 'It—I—it's nothing to do with me.'

'You brought it up,' he reminded her.

Caroline expelled her breath unevenly. 'We'd better go back.' She lifted her head. 'Goodbye—*señor*. I—I hope you have a good journey.'

Luis returned her gaze broodingly, making no move to leave. 'You really believe it, do you not?' he demanded grimly. 'You really accept that I could have a mistress!'

Caroline shook her head. 'I've told you——'

'—it is nothing to do with you, I know. But that is not good enough, *señorita*. I find I do not like to be humoured like a recalcitrant child.'

'*Señor*——'

'No, I will not be treated like this. I am a man, *verdad*! Do you not think that is hard enough for me to try and forget, without you insinuating proof of a relationship that is abhorrent to me!'

'I'm sorry——' Caroline pressed her palms together anxiously, but he was not to be placated.

'Sorry?' he echoed, his eyes smouldering. 'You are always sorry, are you not, *señorita*? Unfortunately, sorry is not always good enough.'

'Oh, Luis . . .'

His name slipped carelessly from her lips, and although she caught her breath at its passing, it was clearly audible. She stood, with lips parted, waiting for the censure she was sure was to come, and with the certain knowledge that her reckless tongue had destroyed any chance of a reconciliation. In any circumstances, she had no right to think of him by his given name, and added to his earlier condemnation it was a total indictment.

Shaking her head helplessly, she turned away, taking deep gulping breaths of air, and as she did so, she felt him move behind her.

'Luis,' he said, and the way he said his name was so much more disturbing than the way she said it. 'You called me Luis,' he added, his breath fanning the nape of her neck. 'You should not have done that.'

'I know, I know,' cried Caroline tormentedly, bending her head over her twisted fingers. 'Oh, why don't you just go away and leave me alone? All right, so I was insolent. Can't you just forget it? You're leaving soon. Does it really matter?'

'It matters to me,' he responded in a low voice, and she started violently when his hands closed on her waist and impelled her back against him.

'What are you doing?' she exclaimed frantically, trying to push his hands away, but then she felt the powerful masculinity of his body moulding itself to hers and her legs almost gave out on her.

'Caroline,' he breathed, rubbing his tongue against the throbbing pulse behind her ear, and her resistance dissolved.

'You—you shouldn't do this,' she protested huskily, but her shoulders were yielding against his chest, her head tipping to one side to accommodate his probing lips. She could feel every hard muscle of his body, and for a few moments it was enough to know that he had forgiven her.

'I know what I should or should not do,' he contradicted her huskily. 'And I do not think my soul will be eternally damned for just holding you in my arms.'

Caroline stiffened at his words, but he would not let her go, and her resistance melted again when his strong hands slid up over her rib-cage to find the rounded fullness of her breasts. They swelled to his touch, the nipples hardening and surging against the thin cotton, and the groan he uttered was one of anguished submission.

'This—I should not do,' he muttered, twisting her round in her arms. 'But I have to,' and before she could make any protest, his mouth sought the trembling sweetness of hers.

Caroline's lips parted beneath the sensuous invasion of his touch, and her conscience was submerged beneath the urgent tide of emotion that swept through her at that moment. Luis's mouth was firm and insistent, hungry in its possession, promoting an intimacy between them that would not be denied. It was a breathtaking, suffocating sublimation of her identity, and her hands groped for him almost blindly. Almost without her volition, her arms were around his neck, her fingers twining in his hair, her nails raking his scalp as she sought to hold him closer. Her whole body was flooded with a feverish excitement, and the intoxicating scents of the garden around them mingled with the musky male scent of his skin, to sensitise her awareness.

It was Luis who eventually pulled away, leaving her with an empty distraught feeling, that threatened to overwhelm her. She felt sick and giddy, seduced by her emotions into a state of complete submission, and his withdrawal left her feeling weak and disorientated.

'So—what do I say now?' he muttered harshly, thrusting savage fingers through his hair. He looked grimly into her drugged features. 'Do I apologise? Do I beg your forgiveness? Or is it too late to pretend I did not want to make love to you?'

Caroline moved her head bemusedly. 'Don't say anything,' she ventured faintly, struggling to regain her own composure, but the angry expletive he used abused her attempt at understanding.

'No?' He spoke violently, and she realised how disgusted he was with himself for allowing this to happen. 'We just forget all about it, is that it?' His face twisted. 'Of course, I forgot. You are an emancipated English girl. You are used to men making love to you. It means nothing to you!'

'That's not true!' Caroline was stung into retaliation. 'I am not used to *men* making love to me!'

'Your lover, then. This man who cares so much about you that he is prepared to allow you to travel half across the world without his protection?'

'Andrew is *married*!' declared Caroline tremulously, wanting to hurt him as he was deliberately hurting her. 'That's why I'm here. That's why he didn't try to stop me!'

Luis's features froze. 'You are in love with a married man?'

Caroline didn't know any more, but she couldn't tell him that. 'What—what if I am?' she countered, and then knew a moment's agony when she saw the real torment in his face.

Shaking her head, she turned away from him, and heard the sound of his footsteps retreating from her. She guessed her words had destroyed any lingering feeling he might have felt for her, and while that knowledge was painful, Luis might take some comfort from it.

CHAPTER SEVEN

THE day after Luis's departure, Don Esteban came to the library while Caroline was giving Emilia her lessons.

It was a day of rain, a steady driving downpour, that ran in rivulets across the windows, and reduced visibility beyond them to nil. It was much different from the rain Caroline was used to, and when it had awakened her that morning, pattering against the window pane, she had lain for several minutes considering how it reflected her mood.

She supposed after every bereavement there was a period of time when one was too numb to really understand the inevitability of what had happened, and Luis's departure was like a bereavement. The knowledge that she might never see him again was too painful to contemplate, and she was living in a state of bemused insensibility, immune to the pangs of physical deprivation.

She had not seen him again after that disastrous scene by the lily pond. As he had predicted, he had been absent for dinner that evening, and the following day at lunch Don Esteban had taken much pleasure and satisfaction in announcing his brother's departure.

'We will all miss him, will we not, *señorita*?' he had remarked, as they took the midday meal together as usual on the terrace, and if there had been any hidden meaning behind his suavely-spoken words, Caroline had been too distraught to notice it.

Yet, for all that, life went on, and although at times the hopelessness of her feelings for Luis and the permanence of their separation was like a massive weight bearing down upon her, she forced herself to behave as she had always done, continually keeping all futile thoughts at bay.

The question of whether or not she would remain at San Luis after her probationary month was up was still far enough distant not to be of any immediate threat, but sooner or later it too would have to be faced. There were times when desperation drove her to think longingly of home, and others, when the thought of leaving Mexico—and putting thousands of miles between her and Luis—filled her with despair. The likelihood that Don Esteban might find her work unsatisfactory was always a possibility, but at least with Emilia she found some measure of relief.

'Tio Vincente is gone,' she said, the morning after Luis's departure, and burst into tears, and comforting the child, Caroline had found comfort herself.

'Why do you call him Tio Vincente?' she asked, after Emilia had dried her tears, and the little girl's chin quivered.

'My mother used to call him Vincente,' she said simply, picking up her pencil again, and Caroline applied herself to the textbooks with a gladiatorial determination.

The advent of Don Esteban was an unexpected diversion. Apart from assuring himself of his daughter's application to work, he had shown little interest in her progress, and Emilia herself looked apprehensive when he stepped into the library. He himself had been absent at dinner the night before, and Caroline had nervously shared the meal with Doña Isabel, but this morning he was as immaculately dressed as usual, only the pouches beneath his eyes bearing witness to a possible over-indulgence.

'Good morning, Miss Leyton, good morning, Emilia,' he greeted them silkily, closing the door behind him and advancing into the room. 'But not such a good morning weatherwise, is it, much more the sort of weather Miss Leyton is used to, I fear.'

Caroline looked up from her books. 'Can I help you, *señor*?' she asked politely. 'Would you like to see how Emilia's work is proceeding? Her English essays are really very good.'

'I am sure I shall have no complaints of your work with Emilia, *señorita*,' her employer assured her smoothly. 'In all honesty, books, and learning, were always a source of boredom for me. I find the practical applications of experience far outweigh the knowledge acquired from books, and while it is important that Emilia should learn these things, they are not the whole meaning of existence, would you not agree?'

Caroline made a helpless gesture. 'If you say so, *señor*.'

'If I say so?' he questioned, coming to stand beside the desk, the pungent fragrance of his after-shaving lotion a sharp assault on her nostrils. 'My dear Miss Leyton, you must agree with me. Why else did you leave the familiarity—the security—of your home in England, if not to gain practical experience?'

Caroline put down her pen and linked her fingers together. She was aware of Emilia, listening to their exchange with an intent expression upon her face, and although Don Eesteban's words seemed innocent enough, she mistrusted his bland assertions.

'In what way can we help you, then, *señor*?' she ventured, endeavouring to appear cool and relaxed. 'If you wish to speak with Emilia, I can easily prepare this lesson elsewhere.'

Don Esteban made a soothing movement, his plump fingers spreading over the desk. 'It is you with whom I wish to speak, *señorita*,' he replied, moistening his thick lips. 'It is a privilege of which I have denied myself, but which I am told has not been denied to others.'

A faint colour invaded Caroline's cheeks. 'What did you want to say, *señor*?' she asked stiffly. 'Naturally, as my employer, you have first call on my time.'

Don Esteban expelled his breath half impatiently. 'Do not be so—touchy, *señorita*! I was not criticising you. I appreciate that while Luis was here your loyalties were divided.'

Caroline froze. 'I don't know what you mean, *señor*.'

'Of course you do.' Don Esteban sighed. 'It was perhaps unfortunate that I was—indisposed on the day of your arrival. Luis's deputation on my behalf enabled him to influence your thinking, and it was natural that you should regard him as your—how shall I put it?—protector?'

'Don Esteban——'

'*Senorita*, I understand. My brother has always had this effect on women. They like him. They trust him. And he always lets them down.'

Caroline drew an unsteady breath. Emilia's eyes were wide now, and the curiosity in their depths was vaguely hostile. She was unlikely to understand what was going on, Caroline guessed, but any criticism of Luis was bound to create antagonism.

'I think this discussion could be concluded at another time, *señor*,' she declared now, casting a meaningful glance in his daughter's direction. 'Perhaps over dinner this evening.' Emilia was always in bed before dinner. 'But now, if you don't mind, we really should get on.'

A brief shadow of impatience crossed Don Esteban's face at her words, but it was quickly dispersed. 'Of course, of course,' he averred placatingly. 'But I think you misunderstand me, *señorita*. I did not come here to discuss my brother. On the contrary, Luis is of no further concern to any of us.' He smiled, his lips curling back with a smugness she only faintly comprehended. 'As it happens, I am driving into Las Estadas this morning, and I wondered if you and Emilia would care to accompany me. As it is such a miserable day, I thought the outing might—divert us.'

Caroline caught her breath. It was the last thing she had expected, and observing Emilia's astonishment, she guessed the suggestion had surprised her, too.

'As it is almost a week since you arrived at San Luis, *señorita*, I thought you might welcome the opportunity of visiting a supermarket, or posting some letters,' her employer continued affably. 'We are so remote here, and it is fitting that you should have some free time.'

'I have plenty of free time, *señor*,' Caroline told him uneasily. 'Emilia and I only work in the mornings, and the rest of the day is my own.'

'But even schoolteachers must have a morning off sometimes,' Don Esteban insisted. 'So? Will you come?'

Caroline looked doubtfully at Emilia. Obviously the child would welcome the outing, and it was true she had written to her parents the night before, but spending several hours in her employer's undiluted company was something else.

'Perhaps—perhaps Emilia would like to accompany you, *señor*,' she faltered tentatively. 'I—er—I have these lessons to prepare——'

Don Esteban's expression hardened. 'Is not my company to your liking, *señorita*?'

'Of course not. I mean—of course it is.' Caroline flushed in embarrassment. 'I just thought——'

'I shall be leaving in fifteen minutes, *señorita*. I suggest you wear waterproof clothing. As you are probably aware, the amenities at Las Estadas leave a lot to be desired!' and without giving her a further chance to protest, he strode arrogantly out of the room.

'You had better get ready, *señorita*,' Emilia remarked, after the door had closed behind him. 'Don Esteban does not like being kept waiting.'

Caroline, whose nerves were feeling decidedly strained, cast her pupil an irritated look. 'Must you call him that?' she exclaimed, shuffling the textbooks together. 'He is your father, Emilia, whether you like it or not. And no amount of wishful thinking will make it otherwise.'

'No, he's not.' Emilia's chin jutted. 'And don't you talk to me in that tone of voice. I know why you are upset. Because Tio Vincente has gone away. But like Don Esteban says, Tio Vincente cares nothing for any woman, since my mother died.'

Caroline felt the first twinges of a headache probing at her forehead. 'You imagine things, Emilia,' she declared, striving desperately for a way to avoid spending the day in her employer's presence. 'And perhaps you should go and change, too. That dress is scarcely suitable for tramping round Las Estadas.'

Emilia shrugged. 'I don't care.'

Caroline sighed. 'Don't you want to go?'

'With Don Esteban? No.'

Caroline shook her head. 'We don't have a choice, do we? Go and get ready. You heard what your father said.'

Emilia gave her a mutinous look as she left the room, but Caroline was too distraught to notice. It was obvious that she would have to go, and after closing Emilia's exercise books, she went to change her shoes.

She was hurrying back along the corridor when Doña Isabel's door opened, and her heart sank when the old lady emerged and spoke to her.

'You are going out, *señorita*? Is that not rather foolish on such a day?'

Relieved to find the old lady was lucid, Caroline forced a smile to her lips. 'Emilia and I are going to Las Estadas with Don Esteban,' she explained. 'Let's hope it may have stopped raining by the time we get there.'

Doña Isabel frowned. 'You are going with Esteban?'

Caroline sighed, hoping this was not going to cause problems. 'Yes.'

Doña Isabel looked at her closely. 'You like Esteban, *señorita*?' she queried. 'I thought Luis said—but no matter. No doubt you know your own mind best.'

Caroline pressed her lips together to stop them from trembling. 'What—did—Don Luis say?' she asked, but already the old lady's mind was wandering.

'You take care, *señorita*,' she warned, and the glitter of her dark eyes caused Caroline's pulse to quicken. 'The Montejos are not to be trusted—as poor Vittoria found out.'

Caroline shook her head. 'Doña Isabel, Don Esteban's mother is dead——'

'Do you think I do not know that?' The old lady was suddenly very erect. 'I know my mind wanders sometimes, but if I confuse Esteban with his father, that is because they are so alike.'

Caroline nodded. It was easier to agree. 'I must be going, *señora*,' she began uncomfortably, and started when the old lady suddenly gripped her wrist with a bony claw.

'Esteban wants you, *señorita*,' she hissed, her breath redolent with a sickly scent of Parma violets. 'Do not ask me how I know. I do. And if you think you will have any choice when the time comes, then you are a fool!'

Caroline tore herself away. 'I think you're imagining things, *señora*,' she declared, though the hand that massaged the reddened skin of her wrist was not quite steady. 'I must repeat, I am Emilia's governess, that is all. Anything else is pure fantasy on your behalf.'

All the same, as she left the old lady to walk quickly along the corridor, Caroline's legs felt decidedly shaky. It was easy enough to tell herself that the old lady was eccentric, inclined towards the very fantasies she had accused her of, nevertheless it was unnerving to be constantly at the mercy of these unwarranted attacks.

Downstairs, Don Esteban was waiting for her, dark and unfamiliar in an oilskin jacket. He looked with approval at her knee-length boots and dark blue mackintosh, then urged her towards the heavy doors with a careless gesture of his hand.

'Emilia——' she said, glancing round anxiously, but there was no sign of her pupil, and her patience wavered. Where was the child? Surely she would not disobey her father. Remembering the last occasion that had happened, Caroline wished she had been more forceful.

'Emilia is not coming,' Don Esteban informed her carelessly, swinging open the outer door and gazing at the drenching downpour. '*Dios mio*, will it never cease?' and without giving her chance to reply, he started down the flight of steps.

'Oh, but—*señor*——' Caroline hastened after him, pulling up her hood as she emerged from the porch. '*Señor*, what do you mean? Where is Emilia? Why isn't she coming with us? If she's not ready, then surely we can wait.'

The Range Rover stood waiting at the foot of the steps, and Don Esteban gazed up at her impatiently. 'Come, *señorita*,' he called, his expression brooking no argument, and with a sigh of puzzled uncertainty Caroline hurried down the steps.

'Emilia——' she said once more, as he bundled her into the front of the Range Rover, and irritation marked the sensual fullness of his lips.

'Emilia is delicate,' he declared, slamming the door and walking round the vehicle to climb in beside her. 'It would not do for her to catch a chill, as she easily might, subjected to the weather. It is better that she remains at home.'

Caroline gazed at him aghast. 'Then isn't it better that I remain here, too?' she protested, as he reached purposefully for the ignition, but Don Esteban merely shrugged his heavy shoulders.

'Just because Emilia is a weakling there is no reason why you should be denied the outing,' he retorted, setting the vehicle into lurching motion, and she realised she had been deliberately tricked into accompanying him.

She stared blindly through the side windows as they drove out of the inner courtyard, then down the drive to the gates. Old Gomez emerged from the lodge to open the gates at Esteban's signal, but although he saluted his employer, there was no sign today of the smile he had reserved for Luis. But then today was hardly a day for smiling, reflected Caroline tautly, unable to forget what Doña Isabel had said. And although she was not alarmed by Don Esteban's behaviour, she was angry, and she saw no reason why he should think he could treat her in this way.

'You seem upset, *señorita*,' he remarked now, as they negotiated the twisting road that led down to the village. 'I thought you would welcome the opportunity to see a little more of my country, in daylight this time, even if the circumstances are not as I could have wished.'

Caroline turned to look at him. 'They are not as I could have wished either, *señor*,' she declared, making no effort to disguise her annoyance. 'I was employed to teach Emilia, not to indulge in sightseeing outings to Las Estadas. You must know that had I suspected Emilia would not be accompanying us, I also should have refused.'

Don Esteban's expression did not alter. 'I see. You would prefer to go back, perhaps?'

'I would prefer to go back,' she agreed.

Don Esteban inclined his head. 'Very well. When we reach the village, I will turn the vehicle round, and we will go back for Emilia.' He made a dismissing gesture. 'And if she contracts a fever, then we must hope she has the strength to overcome it.'

Caroline's lips clenched. 'If Emilia is delicate, it would be madness to take her to Las Estadas on a day like this,' she exclaimed.

'It is your decision, *señorita*,' he intoned flatly, and Caroline gazed at him in helpless fascination.

'You'd do that? You'd take your daughter with us? You'd risk her health——'

'*Señorita*, my wife was like Emilia.' His thick fingers swung the wheel to avoid a pothole in the road, and Caroline groped for the rim of the seat to save herself from falling against him. 'Juana was susceptible to every germ and virus that came her way.' He grimaced. 'Myself, I blame her parents. They used to treat her like glass.' He uttered a short mirthless laugh. 'And like glass, she shattered, without even giving me the son for which I married her. Oh, yes,' this as Caroline turned a disbelieving face towards him, 'that was why I married her, *señorita*. San Luis needed a son and heir, and my father contracted the marriage for me. Unfortunately, he had no idea that it was Luis whom Juana really wanted, when she cast those soulful eyes in this direction.'

Caroline blinked. 'You speak so dispassionately.'

'Why not? Juana never cared for me, and Emilia is like her mother.' He hesitated. 'But perhaps, if I treat her a little less tenderly, she will survive her first pregnancy.'

Caroline expelled her breath with incredulity. '*Señor*, I can't let you do that!'

Don Esteban's heavy lids narrowed his eyes. 'How will you stop me, *señorita*?' he asked, and she could tell he was attracted by the prospect, so that her answer came swift and slightly breathless:

'We will not turn back, *señor*. I will accompany you to Las Estadas.'

It was an arduous journey, the road slippery and running with water, the landscape dark and dripping with rain. Even when the downpour lessened sufficiently to let her see something of her surroundings, the encroaching wall of vegetation was grim and unyielding, giving only on to solid outcrops of rock, starkly chiselled to make way for the road. They passed through areas of cultivated land, where the rampant undergrowth gave way to banana and coffee plantations, and occasionally a cow or a donkey wandered haphazardly into the road, causing Esteban to swerve and swear violently, as the Range Rover's tyres spun uselessly centimetres above the surface. But mostly the journey was accomplished in silence, Caroline too absorbed with what she had learned to pay much attention to Esteban's uncertain humour.

Las Estadas was just as depressing as she remembered it, but this time Esteban parked the Range Rover off the main street, and adjusting his jacket, jumped down into the road.

'I will show you the way to the post office,' he said, walking round the vehicle and swinging open her door. 'Come, I will help you down.' His eyes mocked her. 'I regret there are no sidewalks here.'

Caroline could have done without his assistance, but rather than antagonise him she allowed him to help her down on to the spongy surface of the road. For a moment she was close to him, aware of the flesh-softened muscles of his chest, her lungs filled with the powerful scent of his deodorant, and then she glanced up and found him looking down at her, and recklessly she took a backward step.

Immediately her foot was plunged into the murky depths of a puddle that had formed at the roadside. She tried to disguise her gulp of annoyance, but Esteban saw the consternation on her face; and taking her arm again, he drew her forward.

'Sometimes it is better to bear with the devil we know than tempt the devil we do not,' he remarked, his tongue circling his already moist lips. '*Señorita*, you and I must come to an understanding.' His expression was enigmatic. 'But for now, the post office is this way.'

Caroline bore the intimate possession of his arm about her waist as they crossed the road, but once they were at the other side she determinedly freed herself. She would rather walk in the puddles than have his hands upon her, she thought, revolted by his proprietorial attitude, and she was relieved when the shabby building that housed the post office was reached.

'I have to go to the bank,' Esteban remarked then, glancing thoughtfully about them. 'I suggest you attend to your business here while I am absent, and meet me in half an hour's time at the hotel.'

Caroline's mouth went dry. 'The hotel?' she echoed. 'The hotel where I stayed the night before . . .'

Her voice trailed away, but Esteban didn't appear to notice. 'Allende's *posada, sí,*' he declared shortly. 'We will have lunch there, before returning to San Luis. It is not the most desirable hostelry, I know, but it is the best Las Estadas has to offer.'

Caroline nodded, but her reaction was unmistakable, and as if he was aware of her reticence, Esteban's mouth compressed. 'You find my arrangements displeasing, Miss Leyton?' he enquired heavily. 'Or is the company not to your taste? You would prefer that my brother was here in my place, perhaps?'

Caroline stifled her gasp of astonishment at his words, and forced herself to meet his accusing stare. 'If—if I have given you that impression, I'm sorry, *señor.*'

'Are you?' Esteban was evidently unconvinced. 'Do you dislike me, Miss Leyton?'

'No!' But her denial was almost too quick, too vehement. 'I—er—I'm getting wet, *señor,*' she protested faintly. 'May I go and post my letter?'

Esteban thrust his hands into his coat pockets. '*Muy bien.*' His shoulders hunched. 'Do as you say. We will meet at the hotel in twenty minutes.'

'*Twenty* minutes, *señor?*'

'How long does it take to post a letter?' he countered caustically, and turning, strode away across the muddy street.

The hotel was just as seedy as she remembered, the group of Mexicans sitting on the verandah, tipping back their chairs, as they drank their *tequila* and watched the world go by, just as dead-eyed and indolent. Caroline crossed the slatted boards on hasty feet, reaching the comparative privacy of the reception hall with relief, and then drew back apprehensively, when Señor Allende himself appeared from the bar.

'*Ola*, it is Señorita Leyton, is it not?' he exclaimed, squinting at her in the poor light that filtered through the grimy windows. '*Que quiere usted? Una habitacion?*' He chuckled maliciously. '*No sé si puedo ayudarte.*'

Caroline was about to explain that she didn't understand what he was saying, when her employer's voice interrupted them.

'Miss Leyton does not require a room, Allende,' he stated coldly, coming into the hall behind Caroline, and laying a possessive hand on her shoulder. 'But, had she done so, you would have done well to accommodate her, my friend, unless you are wishing to relinquish the tenancy of this establishment forthwith.'

'*Señor!* Señor Montejo, how could you think such a thing?' The fat little proprietor almost prostrated himself before Esteban. 'Mees Leyton and me—we were having what you call a leetle joke, no?' He cast imploring eyes in Caroline's direction. 'Is that not so, *señorita*? Old Domingo, he likes a leetle fun. You know it is so.'

Caroline wondered how funny it would have been if she had been seeking accommodation, but her conscience would not permit her to be the unwilling instrument of his downfall.

'Señor Allende did—provide me with a room the last time I needed one,' she offered, avoiding the little man's eyes, and Esteban drew a harsh breath.

'So he did. On my recommendation.' His expression was unyielding. '*No obstante*, he would do well to remember to whom he owes his loyalties.'

Caroline thought so, too, judging by the expression on Señor Allende's face. Evidently, Esteban was his landlord, but it was more than just fear of eviction that put that consternation into his eyes. In a town like Las Estadas there could be no future for anyone who fell foul of the Montejos, and she almost pitied the little man as he fawned around them. But when, in the course of his conducting them into the tiny dining room of the hotel and seating them at the best table by the window, she accidentally intercepted Señor Allende's gaze, she was shocked by the fleeting glimpse of hatred she saw there. It was quickly concealed behind a mask of grovelling servility, but the memory of it remained with her, disturbing and unnerving.

CHAPTER EIGHT

ESTEBAN drank too much that evening.

Watching him filling and refilling his glass during dinner, calling for more wine, finishing the meal with a decanter of brandy, Caroline experienced the same kind of discomfort she had suffered on her first evening at the *hacienda*, and now there was no Luis to counteract his indulgence.

But without his brother to taunt and attempt to humiliate, Esteban turned his attention to Doña Isabel, making fun of her pitilessly, mocking her style of dressing, and deriding her husbandless state.

But Doña Isabel just went on spearing cubes of cheese with her knife, and popping them into her mouth. 'If you consider marriage so attractive, Esteban, then perhaps you should consider the success of your own,' she remarked,

nibbling a cracker thoughtfully. 'You have been sin-
gularly unlucky in your partnerships. Your first wife died
without giving you any children at all, and poor Juana
could only produce a puny girl child——'

'*Basta!* Be silent!' Esteban's face convulsed with anger.
'What do you know of anything, you stupid old *bruja*! My
marriage to Margarita was no marriage at all, and Juana
was always a feeble-minded hypochondriac! How could
either of them be expected to give me sons, when they
couldn't even fire a man's passion?'

Doña Isabel shrugged, unmoved by his insults, but
Caroline sank lower into her seat. She had not even
known there had been a wife before the unfortunate
Juana, and she wondered what had happened to her
when her inability to conceive had proved absolute.

'Perhaps it is you, and not Luis, who should enter the
priesthood,' Doña Isabel suggested, and Caroline was
astonished at her audacity. 'After all, Señorita Leyton has
no doubt heard the rumours that Emilia may not be your
daughter, and if that is so, there is no proof that you can
provide an heir for the *hacienda*.'

Caroline thought he was going to hit his aunt then, but
although anger brought the hot colour to his cheeks, and
his eyes almost started from his head, discretion—or perhaps respect for the sharpness of her tongue, which was
more than a match for his—stayed his hand.

'Go to bed, old woman!' he said, sinking back into his
seat, his fingers closing once more around the decanter. 'I
will provide an heir for San Luis soon enough.' His eyes
flickered briefly over Caroline. 'I shall not need Luis's
assistance when that time comes.'

To Caroline's relief, the clouds had disappeared by the
morning, leaving a day that was hot and very humid. But
anything was better than being confined within the walls
of the *hacienda*, and she and Emilia spent the first half of

the morning identifying plants and flowers in the garden. It was Emilia herself who did most of the instruction, teaching Caroline the names of the plants and explaining their cultivation, but the little girl seemed to enjoy airing her knowledge, and Caroline was glad to be out of the heavily cloistered atmosphere.

'Did you enjoy your visit to Las Estadas, *señorita*?' Emilia asked, as they crouched beside the prickly tongues of a cactus, and Caroline gave her charge a thoughtful look.

'You did not accompany us,' she remarked, brushing a leaf from the skirt of Emilia's dress, and the little girl gave a nod of acquiescence. 'I should not have left you, had I known you would not be coming with us.'

Emilia shrugged, and rose to her feet. 'You wanted to go, didn't you? You could have said no.'

'I suppose so.' Caroline straightened, remembering the choice Esteban had given her. 'Well, I'm sorry you were left alone.'

'Oh, I wasn't alone,' retorted Emilia, beginning to walk back towards the house. 'I went down to the stables to talk to Benito. He let me play with Cabrilla. She is the foal of Tio Vincente's mare, Aphrodite, the one he let you use, the day he took you riding.'

Caroline stared at her. 'You know about that?'

'Of course.' Emilia was haughty. 'He told me. But I would have found out anyway. Benito would have told me.'

Caroline sighed. 'I'm not at all sure your father would approve of your spending time down at the stables. Particularly not when you are so prone to colds and chills.'

Emilia's indignation was unmistakable. 'You may be prone to colds and chills, *señorita*, I am not,' she retorted, very much on her dignity. 'And my father would not disapprove of me spending time with Benito. He, too, used to like to visit the stables, when he was a little boy, and later on, he and my mother used to meet there.'

Caroline sighed. 'You're talking about—Don Luis, aren't you?'

'Tio Vincente, yes.' Emilia pursed her lips. 'I've told you, Don Luis is my father. Why do you think he plans to enter the seminary? Because the only woman he ever loved is dead!'

'Where do you find such melodramatic nonsense, Emilia?' Caroline struggled to keep her tone light, even though the child's words were disturbingly plausible. 'Don Luis's mother—your father's stepmother—she has entered the church. It is she, and not your mother, who dictates your uncle's conscience.'

'That's not true.' Emilia stared at her mutinously.

'It is true,' retorted Caroline sharply, annoyed to find she was trembling. 'You must stop imagining things, Emilia. The only person you convince is yourself.'

To Caroline's astonishment, dinner that evening passed without incident. Only the pouches beneath Esteban's eyes looked a little heavier than usual, but his manner towards his aunt had reverted to the patient, sometimes cajoling tolerance he had previously shown. His attitude and conversation were completely different from the night before, and Caroline thought it was almost as if he was two people masquerading in the same body. She had heard that alcohol could change a person's character, but she had never witnessed such a phenomenon until now.

Her own relief was mixed with uncertainty, compounding as it did her doubts concerning her position at San Luis. While the previous evening, she had been convinced that she should leave, as soon as her probationary month was up, tonight her fears seemed groundless, the inevitable result of an over-active imagination. Her sympathy for Emilia, and the confusing identity she was creating for herself, seemed far more important than fending off Esteban's advances, and although she found him looking at her sometimes, with curiously speculative eyes, she suspected his interest had been stimulated by her association with his brother. She doubted he knew the whole truth of that relationship. Indeed, she prayed he did not. And she hoped that now Luis was gone, Esteban's interest in her might wane accordingly.

During the following days, life at the *hacienda* assumed a pattern, and gradually Caroline began to relax. Her mornings were spent working with Emilia, either in the library or the garden, depending on the weather; she rested during the long hot afternoons, renewing her interest in Pope and Steinbeck, from the wide selection available to her on the library shelves. In the evenings she dined with Esteban and his aunt, and discussed the food, and the weather, and the progress Emilia had made that day, and although occasionally she endeavoured to introduce a more stimulating topic, her employer seemed quite content to treat her as he treated his aunt. It was frustrating, after years of being regarded as the intellectual equal of the men she associated with, and she began to realise that Doña Isabel was not as eccentric as she appeared. She had had a lifetime of combating this kind of male dominance, and while it could not be denied that she did occasionally suffer from delusions, perhaps that was the inevitable outcome of a suppressed personality.

The routine was again disrupted by Esteban.

As on that other occasion, he came into the library, and interrupted a biology lesson Caroline was conducting, with the help of a butterfly they had captured in the garden. The glossy-winged creature was safely imprisoned inside an air-filled plastic bag, and Caroline had every intention of letting it go again, once Emilia had had time to examine its complex structure and absorb its various functions. She was in the process of explaining how important its wings were, not only as a means of flight but also as a method of protection, when Esteban came into the room, and for once Emilia turned to her father, in eager exclamation.

'Miss Leyton has captured a butterfly,' she exclaimed, although Caroline noticed she still forbore to address him personally. 'Come and look! Isn't it pretty? Don't you think the colours are beautiful?'

Esteban took up the inflated bag and held it critically towards the light. The insect crawled across the base of the bag, confined within its cocoon of silence, and Esteban's lips curved with mocking satisfaction. 'So. They are a pest,' he observed, his thick fingers curving over the globe, and the helpless creature was thrown into a panic-stricken beating of its wings.

'You're frightening it!' cried Emilia, getting up from her chair and reaching for the bag, but her father held it just out of her reach.

'I should have thought Miss Leyton might more profitably be teaching you about the birds and the bees,' he remarked tormentingly, and the little girl gazed up at him without comprehension.

'The birds and the bees?' she echoed, and Caroline knew she had to intervene.

'Did you want to join our lesson, *señor*?' she asked, firmly taking the imprisoned butterfly out of his grasp and handing it back to Emilia. 'You may find my methods of instruction boring, but you're welcome to listen.'

'I am sure I should enjoy that,' agreed Esteban smoothly, his dark eyes lingering on the dusky hollow between her breasts, just visible above the low vee of her smock dress, and automatically her hand moved to conceal it. 'But that is not why I am here, *señorita*.' He smiled, observing her instinctive gesture. 'It is a fine day—warm and only a little humid. Perhaps you and Emilia would enjoy a visit to the coast.'

'To the coast, *señor*?'

Caroline absorbed this blankly, while Emilia put down the plastic bag and turned to her father eagerly. 'You really mean it?' she exclaimed. 'You will really let us go to Mariposa?' She caught her breath. 'Will you be coming with us?'

'Alas, no.' Esteban's mouth twisted regretfully, but Caroline sensed his inner excitement. She had registered little after that word 'Mariposa', and she guessed his announcement had been deliberate and Emilia's response all he had intended. 'You would like to see the ocean, would you not, Miss Leyton?' he asked. 'It is not far—a matter of fifteen—perhaps twenty miles by road. Tomas will accompany you. Always providing you would like to accept this invitation.'

Taking a deep breath, Caroline chose her words with care. 'If Emilia would enjoy the outing, then naturally I accept. It was kind of you to think of it, *señor*.'

Esteban smiled, but Caroline knew he was enjoying her consternation; she could see it, and she wished she was a little more adept at hiding her feelings. But the news that Luis was only ten or fifteen miles away, across the river estuary, had devastated her. If she had thought of their separation in terms of distance, she had imagined hundreds of miles between them, and to discover that he was so near, and yet so far, was at once painful and incredible.

'You did not know Mariposa was so near, *señorita*?' Esteban probed, and she knew he knew she did not.

'I knew the ocean was not far away,' she responded quickly. 'I can see it, from my bedroom windows. I remember remarking on it to your brother.'

'And he did not tell you how far away it was?' Esteban mocked.

'Oh, yes, he told me,' she answered, and it was nothing short of the truth.

'But not that that was where the seminary was,' Esteban persisted, and Caroline had to shake her head. '*Verdad?* But you can also see the bell tower from your window, *señorita*. A reassuring sight, I am sure.'

Caroline was equally sure it was not, and she wondered what had happened to bring about this sudden reversal in his character. Since the night after their visit to Las Estadas, he had given her no cause for complaint, and if occasionally she suspected he was deliberately playing a role to disarm her, this morning he had certainly abandoned that part.

'So, you will be ready to leave in a few minutes,' he said. 'I will have Tomas fetch the car to the door.'

'Thank you.'

Caroline looked at Emilia's expectant face, and knew she could not disappoint her, but as she went upstairs to repair her make-up she wished she better understood her employer's motives.

It was impossible not to take the time to go to her window, and look out across the stretch of *pampas* to the distant ocean. There was the sea, glistening invitingly on the horizon, and beside it, the dark shape of the bell-tower, which previously had had no significance for her.

Mariposa was as different from Las Estadas as it was possible to be, unless perhaps the fact that the sun was shining made white-daubed houses look quaint instead of shabby. The town was approached by a tree-lined highway, and the main street faced the ocean. A narrow promenade circled the tiny harbour, where fishing boats bobbed on their moorings, and the streets that ran up from the seafront had pinkish-red roofs, and flowers in the window boxes. A tiny market near the harbour offered fish and all kinds of fruit and vegetables, huge juicy melons jostling beside mackerel and whitebait, red snappers and yellowtails.

They had driven to Mariposa not in the Range Rover,

as Caroline had expected, but in an elderly Bugatti,
which Tomas treated with much reverence. He parked
the vehicle now by the harbour, and then turned in his
seat to address his passengers.

He spoke in Spanish, and Emilia, realising Caroline
could not understand, translated: 'He says he has some
shopping to do for Consuelo,' she explained, after listening carefully to his instruction. 'He suggests we—might
like to go for a walk, while he attends to his business.'

'To go for a walk?' echoed Caroline thoughtfully,
glancing about her at the curious faces all around them.
'A walk—where?'

Tomas was beginning to look anxious, and he began
speaking again, more quickly now, gesticulating to Emilia
and spreading wide his hands. Caroline wished she could
understand even half of what he was saying, and she
waited impatiently for the child's explanation.

'It's all right,' said Emilia carelessly, lounging back in
her seat. 'He's only concerned that we should not get lost.
But I told him, I know my way about Mariposa. I shan't
get lost.'

Caroline sighed, and Tomas gazed at her appealingly,
starting to speak again. She thought she caught the word
playa, which she recognised as meaning beach, but apart
from that his rapid chatter meant nothing to her.

'Are you sure he wants us to go for a walk, Emilia?' she
asked, biting her lower lip, and Emilia's jaw jutted.

'I don't tell lies, *señorita*,' she retorted coldly, and Caroline made a placating gesture as Tomas clambered out
of the Bugatti.

Emilia waited until Tomas had been absorbed by the
crowds of people thronging the little market place, before
she pushed forward the front seat, and opening the pas-
senger side door, climbed down from the vehicle. 'Are
you coming, *señorita*?' she enquired, from the roadway,
pulling the straw boater she was wearing firmly down

upon her head, and with a helpless movement of her shoulders Caroline complied.

The sun was hot, but after two weeks Caroline was getting used to its brilliance, and looping the strap of her handbag over her shoulder, she followed Emilia along the salt-pitted promenade. They attracted some curious glances, but they were not accosted, and after a few moments Caroline began to look curiously about her.

She wondered where the seminary was situated, and then guessed it was probably on a rise, which accounted for her being able to see the bell-tower from her window. In consequence, she looked up, and immediately she saw the grey stone walls of a two-storey building, standing on a promontory overlooking the small town.

Her throat went dry as she gazed up at the unmistakable cupola of a bell-tower, and then Emilia intercepted her stare and gave a knowing snort.

'That's not where Tio Vincente stays,' she declared scornfully, as Caroline tore her eyes away. 'That's the Convent of the Sisters of the Annunciation, *señorita*. Where Tio Vincente's mother lives.'

Caroline moistened her parched lips. 'Then where——?'

'Further on. Across the river,' answered Emilia offhandedly. 'If you like, I'll show you where.'

'Oh, I——' Caroline shook her head helplessly. 'I don't think that's a very good idea, Emilia.'

'Why not? You want to see where he stays, don't you?' The little girl's mouth had drawn down. 'Don Esteban thinks so.'

Caroline drew an uneven breath. 'What possible interest could there be for anyone in seeing the grey walls of some religious academy?'

'I don't know,' Emilia shrugged, her face sulky. 'But you asked.'

Caroline sighed. 'I was curious, that's all.'

Emilia looked at her broodingly. 'Didn't you really

know where Mariposa was?' she persisted. 'I wonder why Tio Vincente didn't tell you.'

Caroline endeavoured to appear indifferent. 'I suppose it has nothing to do with me,' she replied, stopping to lean on the harbour wall, peering down into the grey-flecked waters that surged against the rocks. 'We should have brought a shrimping net, Emilia. There are dozens of tiny fish down here, swimming about in shoals.'

Emilia leaned on the wall beside her, but her interest was elsewhere. 'Perhaps he doesn't want to see you, *señorita*,' she remarked doggedly, and Caroline lifted her head to stare at her.

'How could he see me?' she argued, wishing Emilia would leave it alone, then caught her breath when the child replied casually:

'He isn't a prisoner, you know. He sometimes comes into town. Don Esteban knew that when he sent us here. That's why he wanted us to come.'

Caroline had had just about enough. Straightening away from the wall, she faced the child without patience. 'I think you're imagining things again, Emilia,' she declared tautly. 'I've warned you before about the consequences of making up these stories.' She pressed on determinedly, in spite of the little girl's whitening face: 'You've been too long without playmates. People of your own age to mix with. You've become obsessed with things that any normal child would never think of.' She paused, and then finished raggedly: 'You don't need a governess, Emilia. Personal relationships are beyond your comprehension. You should go to school, to a boarding establishment, where you won't have time to worry about your mother or your father, or find ridiculously twisted reasons for a perfectly innocent outing!'

It was a brutal set-down, and Caroline felt an immediate sense of contrition for taking out her own insecurity on the child. As soon as she had finished speaking she wanted to retract her words, but Emilia did not give her a chance to do so.

Her dark eyes wide and wounded in her white face, she turned abruptly away from her governess, and before Caroline guessed her intention, she had darted across the road. Holding her hat on to her head with one hand, the other swinging in urgent motivation, she ran rapidly up the side-street opposite, disappearing swiftly among the lines of drying washing.

It happened so quickly that Caroline was nonplussed. By the time she had gathered her wits and hurried across the road after the little girl, Emilia was nowhere to be seen, and only vacantly staring faces confronted her mute-lipped agitation. If only she knew the language, she flayed herself impotently, then hastened on up the street, hoping that Emilia would change her mind and come back.

Whereas the sun had been only pleasantly hot on their shoulders as they walked beside the harbour, now its rays became a pitiless weapon, beating down on her mercilessly and soaking her limbs with sweat. The simple cotton chemise she was wearing began to cling where it touched her, moulding her skin, and outlining every stimulated curve of her body. She soon tired in the unrelenting heat, and as her footsteps slowed, the glare seemed to envelop and devour her.

'*Señorita?*'

She heard the voice as if from a distance, the waves of light around her seeming to bring its resonance on receding swells of sound. She blinked, but all she could see was the sun striking off whitewashed walls, and smell the pungent odour of dust and heat, and unwashed humanity. She was in another of the narrow streets that opened off one another like a rabbit warren, and her heart raced in panic as she realised how far she had come from the harbour.

'Señorita!'

The summons was repeated, and shading her eyes, she swung about, her legs protesting as she poised herself for flight. She doubted she could outrun anybody in her weakened state, but she would try, even if she collapsed in the attempt.

But, to her astonishment, she found only an elderly man behind her, dressed all in black, with a curious round-brimmed hat upon his head, the crown shallow, and scarcely concealing his wispy threads of hair.

'Puedo ayudar usted, señorita? Se ha perdido?'

Caroline didn't know what he had said, but his manner was gentle, conciliatory, and she expelled the breath she hardly knew she had been holding. 'I'm afraid I don't speak any Spanish,' she ventured, without much encouragement, but the old man nodded, as if he understood.

'Inglesa,' he said, and she understood that. *'Se ha peridido!'*

'I am looking for a little girl,' said Caroline wearily. *'Una niña, señor.'* She put out her hand to indicate Emilia's size. 'She ran away.'

'Una niña, señora? Su hija?'

Caroline blinked. *Hija?* That was daughter, wasn't it? He was asking if the girl was her daughter, and rather than confuse things still further, she nodded.

'A little girl,' she repeated. 'Emilia. Emilia de Montejo!'

'Hah, *Montejo?'* he echoed, obviously recognising that name. 'Emilia de Montejo? *Venga!'*

His bony fingers gripped her forearm, while he indicated that she should go with him, and Caroline glanced about her. The women standing in the doorway of a house opposite were unlikely to help her if she cried for their assistance, but in any case, she doubted the old man could prevent her if she really tried to free herself. She was torn between the awareness that she was lost, and that he might conceivably be trying to help her, and the inevitable possibility that his frailty was just a shield for other men of more dubious appearance. She couldn't forget what Luis had told her about the ever-present threat of a kidnapping, and the idea that Emilia might, at this moment, be in the hands of such men was terrifying.

Yet the old man had seemed to respect the Montejo name, and he looked harmless enough. What else could she do, after all? Return to the harbour without her charge? And no means of communicating with Tomas to gain his assistance!

Shaking her head, she let the old man draw her further into the maze of streets, stumbling as a stone twisted her ankle, dodging the billowing lines of washing. She was so hot and weary, she hardly noticed which way they were going, and while common sense told her, she should keep alert, a numbing lethargy was addling her brain.

When they rounded a corner, and she felt a sudden draught of air on her face, her astonishment was total, and she gazed in amazement at the mudflats of the estuary. Somehow, she didn't know how, they had emerged on to the coast road, and ahead of them lay a narrow bridge over the river.

Her lips parted to make some futile protest, to explain that she would have to go back to find Emilia, when she saw two figures crossing the bridge. One was small and dark, dressed in white, with what looked like a straw boater on her head; while the other was tall and dark, and unmistakably attired in similar robes to her companion.

And suddenly Caroline understood. The man who had rescued her was not some devious villain, but a priest, from the seminary across the river, and he had recognised the name because he knew Luis.

Her eyes darted back to the figures on the bridge, and as they did so, her heart plunged. It was Luis who was holding Emilia's hand, Luis who was returning her charge to her; and the old priest beside her folded his hands in satisfaction.

'*Alli esta su hija, señora!*'

Caroline could have tried to explain then that she was not Emilia's mother, but she was too shocked to do anything but stand and watch Luis and the child as they came off the bridge and along the dusty road towards them. She felt sick with reaction, and weak with relief; but overriding everything else was the painful resuscitation of emotion, and the knowledge that separation would be harder a second time.

The old man greeted Luis warmly, and offered his explanations in his own language. He used his hands a lot in the process, gesturing back towards the streets they had negotiated, pointing at Emilia, and rocking his head expressively from side to side.

Luis's response was curt and concise, the glance he cast in Caroline's direction eloquent of his disapproval. No doubt he blamed her for the whole sorry affair, thought Caroline wearily, and pushed shaking fingers through the damp weight of her hair.

Emilia clung to Luis's hand, avoiding Caroline's eyes, her features still mutinous. Caroline wondered what Luis had thought when the child appeared at the seminary, and acknowledged that in his position she would probably feel angry, too. After all, the little girl must have run a fair distance. Looking across the estuary, Caroline could see the walls of a square building and guessed that was the seminary. But then, she thought, fanning her hot face with a languid hand, Emilia had known where she was going, while she had not.

Eventually the old priest ran out of things to say, and with a sign of benediction he bade them *adios*, trudging off up the road again towards the bridge. Caroline managed to thank him before he went, but he only shook his head in deprecation, wagging his finger at Emilia, as if admonishing her for her recklessness.

Alone with Luis and his niece, Caroline felt completely exhausted, and totally incapable of handling the argument which she was sure was to come. The excitement of seeing Luis again had dissipated in the cold shadow of his disapproval, and although her heart ached in anticipation of his anger, she felt too weary to defend herself.

'Father Enriques tells me you were lost when he found you,' Luis remarked at last, looking at her intently. '*Dios gracias*, he did! You appear to be on the verge of collapse. How did it happen? How did you and Emilia get separated?'

Caroline opened her mouth to protest, then saw Emilia's anxious expression. Obviously the child had not told her uncle the whole truth, and she was waiting with tight-lipped hostility for Caroline to explain what had happened.

But Caroline felt too fatigued to comply. What did it matter, anyway? she thought dully. Emilia had been lost, but now she was found. Let that be an end of the matter.

'Emilia and I were walking together,' she said now, slowly. 'There were a lot of people about and we got separated. I had to look for her.'

Luis's grey eyes narrowed, the long silky lashes shadowing his expression. That he didn't believe her was evident in the glitter in their depths, and the sceptical line of his mouth, but Caroline told herself she didn't care. He was so cold, so remote, so detached from her world, in his long black gown, tied with a plaited cord. A gold cross hung from his belt, and it glinted in the sunlight, reminding her with painful intensity that whatever had been between them was irrevocably over. She told herself she didn't care what he thought of her. She meant nothing to him. But her treacherous senses craved his forgiveness, and yearned for a contact he could not give.

'Where is Tomas?' he demanded now, and Emilia, recovering from her relief at being exonerated of all blame, jerked back her head.

'He parked the car near the market,' she said, permitting a tentative smile in Caroline's direction. 'Miss—Miss Leyton and I didn't want to stay in the car, so we just went for a walk. Like she said,' she finished lamely.

Luis's lips twisted. 'Indeed.' His eyes flickered over Caroline once again, and she became aware of how dishevelled she must look. 'Then I suggest we walk back to the harbour this way,' he indicated the coast road, 'and assure him that you have not disappeared off the face of the earth.'

Emilia nodded eagerly, and Caroline reluctantly straightened herself from her lounging position beside the sea wall. She didn't honestly know if she had the strength to walk back to the harbour, but somehow she would have to do it.

Luis released Emilia's hand, and the little girl ran a little way ahead of them, stopping every now and then to allow them to catch up. Luis walked with Caroline, the movement of his robes causing a faint draught against her bare legs. He seemed taller, more alien than she remembered, but just as disturbing to her emotional condition.

'You realise I do not believe you,' he remarked, in an undertone, his voice low and disruptive. 'You could not simply have become separated. And what is more, Tomas had instructions not to let you out of the car.'

Caroline gasped. 'How do you know that?'

Luis shook his head impatiently. 'It is always so, when Emilia leaves the *hacienda*. Unless Tomas or one of us is with her.'

'I was with her,' pointed out Caroline tautly, but Luis dismissed her presence with a wave of his hand.

'You are no bodyguard, *señorita*.' He made a sound of contempt. 'You cannot even take care of yourself.'

Caroline glanced up at him resentfully. 'Anyone can get lost.'

'Not in a strange town, where they do not understand the language.' His fists clenched. 'Do you know what could have happened to you if Enriques had not happened along?'

Caroline knew, but she would not admit it. 'I can take care of myself, *señor*!' she asserted firmly. 'Just because——'

'Just because—nothing!' he snapped. 'You were—*are*—exhausted! You would have stood no chance at all if some man had taken it into his head to accost you.' He raised his eyes heavenward. 'At least accept the truth for what it is. *Dios mio*, I died a thousand deaths when Emilia arrived at the seminary and told me she had lost you.'

'Emilia did not lose me!' retorted Caroline sharply, then averted her eyes from his accusing stare. 'In any case, I can't believe you were so concerned about me.'

'Can you not?' His fingers tortured the knot of his belt. 'Not even when I tell you I left the seminary without permission?'

Caroline's lips parted. 'Oh, Luis! Luis, I'm sorry. But don't be angry with me, please. I don't think I can stand it.'

She heard his sudden intake of breath, and the shuddering exhalation that followed it. But when he spoke, his voice was low and tormented. 'Why did you come to Mariposa?' he demanded. 'Why did you have to torture me like this? Have you any idea how hard it is for me, living here, knowing you are in Esteban's house?'

Caroline turned her head to stare disbelievingly at him. 'But—your faith——'

'Oh, yes, my faith,' he echoed harshly. 'That is all-important, is it not? Unfortunately, I do not have such faith in my brother!'

Caroline sighed. 'Esteban told me where you were. He—he suggested this outing.'

'He would,' affirmed Luis grimly. 'It pleases him to manipulate people. I just wish to God that you were anywhere else than at the *hacienda*. I do not trust him.'

Caroline frowned, and then assuring herself that Emilia was out of earshot, she said: 'What do you mean? Why don't you trust him?'

'You,' said Luis flatly, causing a prickle of apprehension to feather along her veins. 'I do not trust his reasons for bringing you here.'

'Me?' Caroline shook her head. 'But Señora Garcia employed me——'

'Did she?' Luis sounded unconvinced. 'I wonder.'

'What do you mean?'

'Caroline,' he spoke her name huskily, and her legs felt suddenly weak, 'Esteban has been looking for a so-called governess for Emilia for almost a year. The interviews you attended were not the first. There have been many more, both in England and the United States.'

'But——' Caroline was confused, 'I thought——'

'Señora Garcia may have interviewed you, but ultimately, Esteban had to make the decision.' He frowned. 'Tell me, was there anything unusual about your interview? Did you have to supply any photographs or anything?'

'No.' Caroline tried to think. 'At least, not proper photographs. Señora Garcia did say I ought to get a strip of photographs taken for a visa, but later on——'

'—you didn't need them?'

'No.'

'So what happened to them?'

'I don't know. Señora Garcia kept them, I suppose.'

Luis nodded. 'They were sent to Esteban.'

'How do you know?'

'They had to be.' He expelled his breath heavily. 'It was no accident that you turned out to be so—attractive.'

Caroline made a helpless gesture. 'But why should it matter to him what I looked like?'

'I think you know the answer to that.'

Caroline trembled. 'That's ridiculous!'

'Is it?' Luis gazed broodingly out to sea. 'I wish I could be so sure.'

Caroline touched his sleeve, then drew her fingers away as if it burned her as his moody eyes were turned on her. 'Luis, why don't you come back to San Luis? Why can't you find another vocation? Esteban could employ you on the estate, I know he could. Luis—please——'

'I cannot,' he said tautly, and her spirits plummeted. 'You do not understand, and I do not have time to explain it to you.'

'Find the time,' implored Caroline urgently, as they neared the noisy market square, and she glimpsed Tomas standing by the Bugatti. 'Luis, talk to me. Talk to me, please. You must. You must!'

'I cannot,' he repeated harshly, and her shoulders sagged as Emilia came to possess herself of her uncle's hand once more.

'You will not let Tomas be angry with us, will you, Tio Vincente?' she begged, and her uncle looked down at her resignedly.

'Why should Tomas be angry with you, *pequeña*?' he enquired dryly. 'Unless you disobeyed his instructions. Did you do that, Emilia? Did you lead Miss Leyton into danger?'

Emilia hunched her shoulders. 'Miss Leyton heard what Tomas said,' she said sulkily, but Luis would not allow that.

'Miss Leyton does not understand our language,

Emilia,' he reminded her severely, and then allowed her to clamber inelegantly into the vehicle, while he spoke to the chauffeur in his own language.

Tomas was so relieved to see them, he could only gabble effusively, shaking Luis's hand, and evidently thanking him for restoring his two charges to him. Then Luis turned to Caroline.

'So,' he said, and his voice was unusually thick as he made his formal farewell. 'Look after yourself, *señorita*. And you too, Emilia. I expect you to take care of Miss Leyton on these occasions. And if you promise to do so, I will forgive you.'

Emilia's pale face lost its dejected expression, and bouncing forward on the seat, she leaned out to wrap her arms around Luis's neck. '*Te amo*,' she whispered, hugging him close, and over Emilia's shoulder Caroline saw Luis repeat the child's words.

'Tomas has agreed that he will say nothing of this to Don Esteban,' Luis added, as he put Emilia firmly back into her seat. 'It will serve no useful purpose, and I think Emilia has had enough excitement for one day.'

Caroline nodded, too numb at the prospect of his imminent departure to care one way or the other, and with a stiff nod, he stepped back. '*Vaya con Dios!*'

Caroline bent her head as the Bugatti pulled away, but Emilia turned and waved until her uncle was out of sight. Then she slithered round in her seat and looked half curiously at her governess.

'Didn't you like seeing Tio Vincente again?' she demanded. 'I told you I knew where he was.'

'Yes.' Caroline was finding it hard to say anything. 'But you shouldn't have run away.'

'Well . . .' Emilia shrugged indifferently, 'you were so horrible to me, I wanted to give you a fright.'

'Which you did,' confirmed Caroline tremulously. 'Anyway,' she smoothed the skirt of her dress, 'I suggest we forget all about it now. So far as your father is concerned, we had a pleasant outing, and we didn't meet anyone.'

Emilia bent her head. 'Tio Vincente really likes you, doesn't he?' she persisted, causing Caroline's nails to dig into her palms. 'He was really upset when I told him I didn't know where you were.'

'Emilia, stop it!' Caroline's nerves were almost at screaming pitch. 'Let's drop the subject. I never want to see your uncle again.'

Emilia's speculative gaze said she didn't believe her, and Caroline couldn't altogether blame her. She knew she must look as sick as she felt. But she could not allow Esteban to suspect that anything was wrong, especially after what Luis had told her. It would be easier if she went home, she thought, crushing the sense of despair that filled her at this admission. To go on hoping was just a foolish whim, and the longer Luis was at Mariposa, the more remote her dreams became. Better to go, to make a clean break when her month was up, to sever for ever any chance of meeting him again.

She refused to consider the possibility that Esteban might not let her go. How could he stop her? she asked herself reasonably. She was a free woman, a British citizen; any coercion on his part would not be tolerated.

And yet, when she arrived back at the *hacienda*, the first place she looked was the library. Leaving Emilia to regale her father and Doña Isabel with the details of their outing, she entered the booklined room in search of the butterfly she had left imprisoned.

She did not have to look far. Someone, she had no way of proving who, had pierced a hole in the plastic bag, allowing all the air to escape. The butterfly was dead, its wings spread in its final battle for survival.

CHAPTER NINE

IT was foolish to let the death of a butterfly upset her, but it did, and she could hardly bring herself to go downstairs again and face her employer. She had fled to her room after finding the pathetic corpse still lying in its plastic shroud, and even after washing her face and brushing her hair, she was still in a state of shocked bemusement.

She knew that seeing Luis like that was the real agony, but nothing could alter the fact that she had been responsible for the butterfly's cruel demise. It was the manner of its death that troubled her most. If someone had crushed the insect, or trampled it to death, she might have understood. But to cold-bloodedly rob a living creature of air, so that every panic-stricken beat of its wings decreased its chances of survival, was the essence of a very subtle kind of cruelty.

Of course, she acknowledged, viewing her pale face in the mirror without satisfaction, she could be wrong. Esteban might have had nothing to do with it. There might, conceivably, have been a hole in the bag before they left. But none of these possibilities convinced her, and she went down to lunch feeling sick and uneasy, and just a little frightened.

But as if the morning had never been, Esteban was the soul of consideration and politeness. Assisting Caroline into her chair at the glass-topped table laid on the terrace, overlooking the pool with the stone jaguar, he set an iced fruit juice in front of her, then proceeded to discuss her outing with a geniality that quite disarmed her.

'Emilia tells me you did not have time to go to the beach, *señorita*,' he remarked, helping himself from the

tray of canapés placed beside him, and Caroline acknowledged the conspiratorial look the little girl cast in her
direction. 'But you did see the market at Mariposa, and
the harbour, so perhaps you can go to the beach another
day.'

'Perhaps,' agreed Caroline noncommittally, sipping the
freshly-squeezed orange juice. 'But I really think Emilia
learns more from lessons than outings, *señor*. And I'm sure
you want her to achieve the best qualifications possible.'

Esteban smiled, his thick lips greasy from the meat
oozing from the rolled banana leaf he just put into his
mouth. 'I am sure we are all satisfied with your progress,
señorita,' he responded, licking his fingers. 'I have never
known my daughter enjoy her lessons so much.'

'You're very kind.' Caroline forced a faint smile, but
the conversation was not going at all the way she had
intended. 'However,' she added carefully, 'it has to be
said that Emilia might benefit more from a more formal
education, *señor*.'

Fortunately, Emilia had gone to feed the fish and was
not listening to their conversation, but Doña Isabel had
heard her words, and now she said: 'You see, Esteban.
Señorita Leyton's ideas are—radical. I said as much
before, if you remember?'

Esteban shook his head, ignoring the old lady. 'Emilia
will not be going to university, as you did, *señorita*,' he
told Caroline pleasantly. 'Therefore there is no need for a
more—formal education.'

Caroline took a deep breath. 'Nevertheless, I wonder if
you realise how lonely your daughter is, *señor*? I mean,
she has no playmates, no one of her own age to associate
with at all. Don't you think she might benefit from the
friendship of children of her own age?'

Esteban raised his wine glass to his lips, studied her
across its rim for a moment, then set it down again. 'But
this is amusing, *señorita*,' he exclaimed, and gave a short

laugh, as if to prove it. 'Anyone would think you wanted to be dismissed!' He moved his shoulders expressively. '*Señorita*, I am quite satisfied with the method of Emilia's education, and if you are so worried about her—isolation from children of her own age, then I am prepared to make a further concession.'

'You are?' Caroline spoke faintly.

'But of course.' Esteban frowned. 'The Calveiros—you remember the Calveiros? Their eldest daughter is married and lives only a few miles from Las Estadas. She has two children nearing Emilia's age, a boy and a girl. I suggest I invite them to share lessons with Emilia, if you have no objections, and afterwards there will be time for play before they have to go home.'

Caroline felt weak. 'I—I have no objections, *señor*. If—if that's what you want——'

'It is what I want, *señorita*,' Esteban assured her firmly, and for the moment there was nothing more Caroline could say.

He was as good as his word. The following week Victor and Juanita Alvarez joined Caroline's morning classes, and in the effort required to bring them up to Emilia's standard, Caroline had little time to worry about her own difficulties.

Victor was older than Emilia, but at ten, he did not have her grasp of languages. Juanita was the same age, but was quite backward in both writing and reading, and Caroline spent hours teaching her how to do the simplest kind of arithmetic.

Still, she acknowledged, it was good for Emilia. Because of her advanced abilities, she was able to help Caroline with Juanita, and her own superiority increased her confidence a hundredfold. She and Victor almost came to blows half a dozen times during that first week, but gradually they all settled down.

It was revealed that their mother had been teaching

them up to this point, but that in six months' time Victor was to go to the convent school in Merida. Juanita would join him there, when she was older, and Caroline wished Esteban would let Emilia go there, too. But he seemed determined to keep Emilia at home, and Caroline shrank from broaching the subject of her departure.

There were no more outings to Mariposa, but one evening Esteban suggested Caroline might like to join him for a ride the following morning. 'Not on horseback, you understand,' he said, as she was struggling to find some reason to refuse, 'I do not like horses, but in an open carriage I use to drive about the estate.'

'But—the children——' began Caroline doubtfully. 'Their lessons——'

'We will be back before it is time for lessons,' retorted Esteban shortly, and she decided it would be easier to give in.

The next morning, however, she regretted her submission. The idea of sharing with Esteban something she had previously only shared with Luis filled her with reluctance, and the lowering skies above them seemed to emphasise her inhibitions.

The trap, for it was little more, awaited them at the stables, with the mare Caroline had ridden tethered between the shafts. Old Benito gave Caroline a dubious look as she climbed into the carriage beside her employer, but he refrained from commenting, aside from a muffled grunt in answer to Esteban's greeting. It was obvious that he, like Gomez, saved his affection for Luis, and she couldn't help wondering why their father had not divided the estate between his sons. It seemed so unfair that one should have all and the other nothing, but perhaps the law of primogeniture prevailed.

In spite of her apprehensions, it was good to be out on the *pampas* again, though she still viewed the cattle with some unease. Riding in the carriage was not like being on horseback, and although that had scared her too, she had known she could outrun them if she had to.

However, Esteban showed no such misgivings. On the contrary, he drove through the herd without hesitation, and stopped to speak to the drovers before driving on.

His destination was a knoll overlooking the swirling waters of the river, and after securing the reins, he suggested they got down and walked for a while. 'The ground may be spongy, but you're wearing boots,' he observed when Caroline hung back, and with a fatalistic feeling Caroline accepted his hand.

He did not release her fingers, however, after she was safely on the turf beside him, and after a moment's futile effort, she had to voice her objection. 'Please—let me go, *señor*,' she begged him stiffly, and when he still did not do so, she added: 'Really, I'm quite capable of walking by myself.'

'I am sure you are, *señorita*,' he remarked, raising her resisting fingers to his lips. 'But I enjoy helping you, and I shouldn't like you to run away.'

'There's no likelihood of that here, is there?' Caroline exclaimed, annoyed at the sudden tremor in her voice. 'Please, *señor*, you're upsetting me. Have—have the goodness to release my hand.'

'Very well.' Esteban obediently let her go, and she immediately pushed her hands into the pockets of the short leather jacket she had put on over dark green corded trousers. She was hardly surprised to find her palms were moist, or that the back of her neck felt damp, but her relief was so great she could dismiss these other symptoms of her apprehension.

They walked a short way, Caroline a few steps behind her employer, then Esteban stopped again and turned to her. There was the lick of rain in the air, a heaviness evident in the ominous-looking clouds on the horizon, and she thought for a moment he was going to suggest they turn back. But instead of this, he faced her, squarely across her path, and as she faltered in hesitation he said:

'I suppose you are aware that in a few days your probationary month with us will be up?'

Caroline expelled her breath unsteadily, aware that she had been expecting something more than this, but his question demanded an answer, and she strove to give it composedly.

'I—I am aware of it, *señor*,' she said, endeavouring to hide her stammer. 'It—it's been on my mind, as a matter of fact. The decision I have to make.'

'The decision?' Esteban regarded her intently. 'What decision do you have to make, *señorita*? Surely the decision is mine.'

Caroline cleared her throat. 'Well, yes. Yes, it is. But it's mine, too, *señor*. The—the probationary period is on both sides.'

Esteban's dark brows descended. 'You are not serious, *señorita*?'

'Oh, but I am.' Caroline licked her lips. 'It—it was a big decision for me to make, *señor*, coming out here, leaving my home and my family. I—I had to try it, to see if I was happy here. There was no other way.'

'And?' Esteban waited grimly for her answer.

'And—well——' Caroline was finding it increasingly difficult to go on. An image of Emilia's small face was imprinted on her mind, appealing to her, reproaching her, and although she told herself that if she was not there Esteban would have to consider the convent school, she dreaded the retribution he might take on the child.

'And what if I do not accept your decision?' Esteban suggested suddenly, interrupting her troubled thoughts.

'You—want me to leave, *señor*?' Caroline held herself tensely.

'No.' His response was what she had been afraid of.

'No, I do not wish you to leave—Caroline.' His use of her name made the hairs on the back of her neck prickle now. 'I want you to stay. For always.'

Caroline's lungs felt constricted, and she gazed at him disbelievingly. 'I—beg your pardon——'

'You heard what I said, *querida*.' He took a step towards her, which she quickly nullified by taking a step backward. 'I want you to remain at San Luis. Not just as Emilia's governess, but as my wife!'

'You—you don't mean that!'

Caroline turned her back on him in an effort to gain some time, but Esteban was adamant.

'I do mean it. I mean every word of it.' His knuckles traced the paling hollow of her cheek. 'Do not look so alarmed. It is quite a compliment I am paying you.'

Caroline shook her head, flinching away from his touch as if it repelled her. Which it did—just as he did. Like a snake! She fought for reason, trying to think coherently through the haze of disbelief and blind panic that fogged her brain. But all she could think of was her helplessness and her vulnerability, and the isolation of her situation here at the *hacienda*.

'What is the matter, *querida*?' Esteban was not blind, and her reaction to his proposal was all too evident. 'Surely Luis warned you of my determination to have a son? I cannot believe that during those—intimate conversations you had with him, he did not confess his hope that one day San Luis de Merced might be his!'

'No!' Caroline was appalled. 'No, he has never——'

'But you did realise that if I could not provide an heir, the estate would revert to my brother?'

'I never thought about it.' Caroline made a frustrated gesture. 'It has nothing to do with me.'

'Oh, but it does.' Esteban stepped towards her again, and this time his hands on her shoulders prevented her from backing away from him. 'Caroline, do not look so

anxious. I am not threatening you. And naturally, I realise you need time to think it over.' He drew her in-
exorably towards him, his dark eyes hypnotic in their
intensity. 'But do not take too long. I am not a patient
man, and you must understand, I am eager to tell the
world of my good fortune.'

His words brought her to her senses. With a determined jerk she was free and facing him bravely. 'I
can't,' she said, and there was a desperate note in her
voice. 'I can't marry you, *señor*. I don't love you, and
although I realise that isn't a necessary attribute in your
country, it generally is in mine.' She took a deep breath.
'I—er—naturally, I'm flattered.' She swallowed the lie
with some effort. 'But I'm afraid I have to refuse.'

Esteban made no immediate response, and as they
stood there, facing one another, the rain began to come
down. It fell heavily, huge globules of water that could
soak a man in seconds, pattering noisily on the seats in
the carriage, whispering in the grass about their feet.

It quickly soaked Esteban's dark hair, running in rivulets down his forehead and into his eyes. He cursed irritably, raking back his hair with a careless hand, then
glanced angrily round at the carriage.

'We'd better go back,' suggested Caroline cautiously,
half relieved by the advent of the storm. At least, it had
cut short Esteban's protests, she thought, and leaving
him, she stepped tentatively across the grass towards the
carriage.

Esteban overtook her before she had taken half a dozen
steps, passing her aggressively, climbing into the two-
wheeled vehicle, and releasing the mare's reins. The little
carriage lurched forwards, as the first clap of thunder re-
verberated ominously across the plain, and Caroline
started to run as she realised what he was about to do.

'Wait!' she exclaimed, stumbling as she ran, wiping the
blinding torrent out of her eyes, but Esteban ignored her.

With reckless abandon he whipped up the mare, setting her at a gallop, leaving Caroline to gaze after him with a sickening sense of disbelief.

The carriage soon disappeared into the mist that shrouded the plain, and hid the *hacienda* from her sight. Even the herd of cattle was invisible, somewhere between her and safety. She was at least two miles from her destination, rapidly getting soaked to the skin, with the certain knowledge that Esteban would send no search party out to look for her.

Panic threatened to overwhelm her. It would be so easy to give in to the tears that were pricking the backs of her eyes, and succumb to a sense of despair. But she knew, if she allowed herself to give up, if she stayed where she was, and waited until someone came to find her, she could well die of pneumonia or exposure or both, and although she felt desperate, she was also furiously angry.

Feeding this anger, realising it was the only thing likely to keep her going, she set off across the plain, in the direction from which she thought they had come. The ground, already spongy before the downpour, was a quagmire, but although her legs ached with every step she took, she persevered.

It was the smell of the cattle that alerted her to their proximity, and her nerve almost gave out on her when a group of the beasts loomed up in front of her. She realised how helpless she was, without even a mount to save herself on, and she wondered if she had any chance of coming through them unscathed. What if she missed her way? What if she trudged round in circles, unable to find her way back until the rain stopped? It was frightening how unfamiliar things could seem when there was no landmark to cling to.

The thunder rumbled again, accompanied by a searing flash of lightning, and the cattle stirred in protest. Caroline was terrified. She knew storms had been known to stampede a herd, and her own position among them was hopelessly reckless. But this was the way they had come. She knew of no other way. And did she really have any choice?

Ignoring her fears, she pressed on, avoiding the brooding brown eyes raised to watch her passage and praying that the animals would pay her no heed. It seemed hours since she left the knoll beside the river, and the rain just kept on coming down and down. Her trousers were soaked, her boots squelched with water, and the shoulders of her jacket were heavy with moisture. Her hair was plastered to her head, and although she was sure it was dripping down her neck, it was all one with the drenching cascade of the storm.

The ferocity of another flash of lightning caused her to make a little sound of alarm, and the cattle nearest to her shifted restlessly. Caroline clapped her hand over her mouth, silencing any further sound she might make, and stumbled on tearfully, her legs weak and unsteady. She was not going to make it, a small voice inside her taunted, and in all honesty she was beginning to wonder if she could.

The low murmur of voices when it came to her seemed like an extension of her own inner protest. It came to her ears through the steady tumult of the rain, mingling with the movements of the cattle, the lowing sounds they made as they shifted from one grazing spot to another.

She halted uncertainly, half afraid she was having hallucinations, but there was definitely someone within calling distance. The trouble was, she was afraid to call for fear of alarming the cattle, and straining her ears, she endeavoured to move in the direction from which the voices had come.

The sound receded, and devastation gripped her. Was she going in the wrong direction? Had she somehow missed her way in her haste to make contact with another human being? Were sounds distorted by water, deflected by so many solid objects?

She realised she was moving with more confidence through the cattle, actually forgetting her fear of them as she strove to reach her goal. She no longer started every time a horned head was turned in her direction, and she told herself with determination that she was going to make it.

When the flash of lightning illuminated the bivouac beneath the trees, she could hardly believe it. Someone had stretched a waterproof sheet between two branches, and beneath its improvised shelter she stood, shaking with reaction.

She was alone, but the evidence of recent occupation was all about her. A metal coffee-pot simmered on the ashes of a fire, and there was the smell of fresh meat and cornbread. Obviously the drovers had been having breakfast, and the voices she had heard had come from here.

Bending down, she groped for a metal cup, and ignoring the dregs in the bottom, poured hot coffee into it. Then, still crouched down, she raised the cup to her lips, shivering as the steaming liquid ran warmly into her stomach.

'*Ola, que quiere usted?*'

The harsh male voice that accosted her brought her head up with a start, and she got unsteadily to her feet. The rainwater had darkened her ash-fair hair, but as the man looked at her, her identity was unmistakable, and his moustachioed lips parted in an expression of ludicrous disbelief.

'*Señorita!*' he exclaimed, and then, as another man followed him into the shelter, he turned to him to speak in a garbled *patois*.

Caroline could not understand what they were saying, but she was so relieved to have found shelter, she hardly cared. Her limbs ached, and she was soaked to the skin, and sooner or later she would have to come to terms with Esteban's abandonment of her, but right now she could only be grateful for another human's company.

The men turned to her then, and spoke in slow careful Spanish. '*Que hay? A donde va usted? Donde esta* Don Esteban?'

Caroline faced them wearily. She guessed, after recognising Esteban's name, that they were asking where he was. Perhaps they thought she had abandoned him, she mused half hysterically, then forced herself to speak calmly as she tried to make them understand.

'Don Esteban—er—a—*hacienda*,' she said. 'You—take me—there?'

She gestured as she spoke, pointing to herself, then out into the rain, she hoped towards her destination.

The men looked troubled. Obviously they were concerned that Don Esteban was not with her. Maybe they imagined she had thrown him into the river, she thought, feeling weak at the thought of having to go and look for him.

They held a whispered conference, arguing together, glancing frequently in her direction, evidently deciding whether or not to believe her. Caroline waited heavily, the weariness of reaction coming over her, and she gazed at them bleakly when they eventually touched her arm.

'*Venga, señorita,*' one of them said encouragingly, gesticulating towards where their horses were tethered, and with a sense of inevitability Caroline followed the man outside.

The rain was lessening slightly, although the thunder still rumbled in the distance. The storm was abating, and with it came the tremulous awareness of having to face her employer with her resignation.

She was given a mount, a spirited palomino, that was more accustomed to rounding up stray cattle than being bridle-led across the *pampas*. Caroline clung on tightly, unable to decide in what direction they were going, and wondered rather headily what she would do if the men proved unreliable. If they had recognised her, it was unlikely that anything unpleasant would befall her, she consoled herself. Her own experiences of Don Esteban had proved that he was not a man one crossed lightly.

When the horses began the ascent to the gates of the *hacienda*, she could hardly believe it. She was safe, she thought joyfully, then revised that opinion. She was back at the *hacienda*, that was all. She had still to stomach whatever manner of retribution Esteban might devise for her refusal.

Gomez opened the gates and gazed at her in astonishment. The words he exchanged with the man accompanying her apparently gave him no satisfaction either, and Caroline's head ached from trying to piece together what was being said. Something about Esteban, she hazarded, feeling totally exhausted, and she could hardly swing her legs across the saddle, when they reached the shallow flight of steps.

The door was opened almost as soon as she had dismounted, and as on the occasion of her arrival at San Luis, Consuelo appeared at the head of the steps.

Her shocked exclamation was intelligible in any language, and she hurried down the steps urgently, uncaring of the persistent drizzle. She caught Caroline about her waist, as her legs buckled beneath her, and with the aid of one of the maids she summoned, they half carried Caroline into the house.

What happened next was just a blur to the exhausted girl. She was aware of hands supporting her as she climbed the stairs to her room, of other hands stripping away her clothes, and the painful protest of chilled limbs suddenly thrust into warm water. No one mentioned Esteban, and she wondered if he knew she was back. But not until she was wrapped in warm towels did Doña

Isabel appear to ask questions.

'You are feeling better?' she enquired, waving away the girl who had been towelling Caroline's head with an imperious hand. 'The servants tell me you came back alone. That Esteban was not with you. Would you like to tell me where he is?'

Caroline gasped. 'He's not back!'

'That is what I said.' Doña Isabel arched her thin brows. 'What happened? Was there an accident? Has Esteban been hurt?'

The dispassionate tone of this enquiry chilled Caroline's blood, and yet remembering how Esteban had tormented his aunt, she could hardly blame the old lady. 'I don't know where he is,' she exclaimed, plucking anxiously at the soft bathsheet. 'He—he—we got separated. I assumed he had come back here.'

'But now you know he did not,' retorted Doña Isabel sharply. 'What took place between you? I presume there was some—*contretemps?*'

Caroline felt an hysterical desire to laugh. 'You—could put it like that,' she admitted huskily. 'He—he asked me to marry him, *señora.*'

Doña Isabel showed no surprise, but then why should she? thought Caroline wearily. She had suspected this all along. Instead, she folded her gnarled hands tightly together and walked stiffly across to the windows.

'You did not accept.' It was a statement, and Caroline conceded the point. 'He was angry.'

Caroline sighed. 'He drove away and—and left me.'

Doña Isabel made a sound of impatience. '*Idiota!*' she mouthed grimly. 'You could have been trampled to death!'

Caroline bent her head. 'You don't think——'

'No.' Doña Isabel turned to her. 'Esteban has more sense than that.' But she frowned all the same. '*No obstante*, his absence is a cause for concern, and I have instructed a search party to investigate immediately.'

Caroline acknowledged this silently.

'So, *señorita*?' The old lady was very much in control. 'You will be leaving San Luis?'

Caroline nodded.

'It is for the best,' Doña Isabel agreed. 'Esteban would be better to turn his attentions towards Señorita Calveiro. She, at least, would know what to expect.'

It was lunchtime before Esteban was found and brought back to the *hacienda*. Apparently the carriage had overturned in the mud, and like Caroline, he had been forced to walk back. Unfortunately, it appeared he had walked in the wrong direction, and remembering how angry he had been, Caroline was not truly surprised. However, he was soaked to the skin, as she had been, and chilled by the length of his ordeal, and she watched through a crack in the library door as he was helped up the stairs.

Emilia, ever-inquisitive, discovered from Consuelo that the doctor had been sent for, and Caroline was relieved when he did not appear for either lunch or dinner. She herself was still very much shaken by what had happened, and it was enough to have to answer Emilia's questions.

She dreaded having to tell the child that she was leaving. Although they were not close, a certain *rapport* had sprung up between them, and given time, she felt sure they would have become firm friends. But that was impossible now, she had to accept it, and she waited apprehensively for the moment when Esteban learned of her decision.

CHAPTER TEN

THE following morning Caroline awakened with a sore throat and a snuffly nose. She guessed her soaking the previous day had made her susceptible to the virus, and she was unutterably relieved to discover that the previous day's storm had made the roads so bad that Victor and Juanita would not be attending lessons. Emilia was sorry she was not to see her playmates, but sympathetic to Caroline's condition, and the morning passed without incident within the quiet walls of the library.

At lunchtime, Caroline steeled herself to face her employer, only to find her efforts had been futile. Esteban was still indisposed, and Doña Isabel seemed curiously unwilling to discuss his condition.

'He will send for you when he wishes to see you, *señorita*,' she declared, spearing a sweet potato on her fork, and Caroline could only feel relief at this second, unexpected, reprieve.

'Why did you not come back with him?' Emilia asked again, as she and Caroline were leaving the morning room. 'I thought you had been out alone, but Consuelo said you went out together.'

Caroline sighed. 'We—we had an argument, and I decided to—to walk back.' She crossed her fingers. 'Then it started to rain.'

Emilia accepted this without comment, but Caroline could see she was not completely satisfied. However, she did not pursue the subject, and Caroline delivered her into the hands of a nursemaid before making her own way to her bedroom.

Esteban did not appear at dinner either, and there was

a curiously expectant atmosphere about the household that Caroline had not noticed before. Maybe they were more concerned about their master's health than she knew, she mused thoughtfully, but they had never previously given her that impression.

She went to bed early, her cold symptoms coalescing to give her a throbbing headache, and slept almost immediately, drugged by the aspirin she had taken in some water.

She awakened to a darkened room, and blinked for a moment, wondering what, or who, had aroused her. Switching on the lamp beside her bed, she examined the hands of her watch. It was only a little after one o'clock, and she had slept for a matter of only three or four hours. She doubted she would have woken without any reason— at least, not for another three or four hours.

Sliding out of bed, she pushed her feet into soft mules and groped for the satin wrapper that matched her nightdress. It was useless to pretend she was not now completely alert, and she decided she would read for a while before attempting to sleep again.

But first she opened the door into the corridor and peered out tentatively, listening for any sound. The lights in the corridor were still on, which was unusual, she thought, and leaving her bedroom door ajar she tiptoed along to Doña Isabel's room. Perhaps the old lady was sick, she thought. Perhaps she had cried out. Whatever her opinion of Doña Isabel, she would not like to think of her lying there, helpless, when she was only a few feet away.

She put her ear against the panels, straining to hear any irregular note in her breathing, then almost fell over when the door was suddenly opened, and she was catapulted into the room.

Recovering herself with as much dignity as she could muster, she opened her mouth to apologise to the old lady, sitting up in the square four-poster bed. But then she realised it was not Doña Isabel who had opened the door, and her eyes darted swiftly to the tall man standing to one side of her.

'*Luis!*' she breathed, half convinced she really was hallucinating this time, and his dark face convulsed in a spasm of emotion. But before he could say anything Doña Isabel interposed, her appearance curiously vulnerable, without the elaborate coiffure she usually affected.

'What do you think you are doing, *señorita*?' she demanded severely, pointing an imperious finger. 'How dare you stand listening at my door? You told me you had a headache, that you were going to take some medication and have an early night. How long have you been eavesdropping on our conversation?'

'I didn't. I mean—I haven't.' Caroline glanced helplessly at Luis, appealing for his assistance, but he seemed like a stranger to her. 'Doña Isabel, someone—something—woke me up. I—I thought you might be ill——'

'And you came to find out?' suggested the old lady sceptically.

'Yes.' Caroline sighed. 'I'm sorry if I'm intruding.' Her hand went nervously to the neckline of her robe. 'I—I apologise. If—if you'll excuse me——'

She turned back into the corridor, intent only on putting herself out of their sight, but as if suddenly galvanised, Luis came after her then, excusing himself from his aunt with a gesture, and closing the heavy door behind him. 'Wait!' he said. '*Señorita*, wait!' And then, more heavily: 'Caroline, do not shut your door against me. I must talk to you.'

Caroline halted in the doorway to her room. 'Well?' she said tremulously, viewing his dark-robed figure without approval. 'You don't have to worry, you know. I did not eavesdrop on your conversation. I really did think your aunt might have called out, or I shouldn't have left my room.'

Luis sighed, supporting himself with one hand against the wall beside the door and massaging the back of his neck with the other. 'I have not said I disbelieve you, have I?' he argued, meeting her indignant gaze. 'The door to my aunt's room slammed in the draught. That is probably what disturbed you. I offer an explanation.'

Caroline nodded. 'Very well, you've solved the problem. Now you can go back to your aunt and continue your secret discussions——'

'They are not secret discussions,' Luis interrupted her impatiently, but Caroline would not have that.

'What would you call them then?' she demanded. 'You come here at the dead of night, obviously so that I—so that *no one*—knows you're here——'

'You do not understand.'

'No, I don't. And I don't want to. If you'll let me close my door——'

'Caroline, stop this!' His expression had hardened into a taut mask. 'You have no right to behave as if I had committed some crime! I am here at my aunt's invitation——'

'I don't want to know why you're here,' she retorted, too hurt and too confused to care what she said. 'Go back to your seminary. I'm leaving anyway. In a few days I'll be back home in England, among people who live simple, ordinary lives——'

'And with this man who already has one wife?' enquired Luis grimly, and the small spurt of resistance went out of her. With her lips pressed tightly together she turned away, shaking her head as she did so, and after a swift confirmation that the corridor behind him was empty, Luis stepped into the room after her and closed the door.

Caroline turned as the latch clicked into place, and caught her breath in disbelief when she saw Luis just inside the door. 'What do you think you're doing?' she exclaimed, half troubled by his strained expression, and he rested back against the panels, probing his temples with finger and thumb.

'We have to talk,' he got out harshly, closing his eyes for a moment, as though the knowledge pained him. 'There are things you must understand, before you judge me so uncharitably.'

Caroline drew a deep breath, feeling the need to justify herself. 'I—I'm not judging you,' she said, 'I just don't want to be involved!'

'Is that true?'

He looked at her then, the grey eyes bleak with some dark emotion, and her lids fell before his. 'You know—it's nothing to do with me,' she said, choosing her words with care. 'This—this family is not my concern——'

'And hasn't my brother made it so?' demanded Luis roughly, straightening away from the door, so that he towered over her like some avenging spirit. 'Is it not true that Esteban has asked you to be his wife?'

Caroline looked up. 'Well, yes. But I refused——'

'And you think that will be the end of it? Your refusal?' he sneered. 'You are so innocent in some ways, *señorita*!'

Caroline stiffened her spine. 'I don't know what you mean.'

'I think you do.' Luis drew an impatient breath. 'Oh, Caroline, I know my brother. He is sick at present, but when he gets better——'

'—I shall be gone,' said Caroline, with trembling dignity. 'Are you trying to frighten me, *señor*? Because I should tell you, I do not scare so easily.'

Luis sighed, shaking his head. 'As when you walked home through the cattle?' he suggested. 'That was brave, *si*. But human beings are not so predictable as cattle.'

Caroline sought the bedpost, clinging to it with both

hands. 'What are you trying to tell me, *señor*? What do you want to say? It's late, and—and I'm tired. And I know you didn't come here to see me!'

'You do not know anything,' responded Luis tightly. 'However, you are right, this is not the time or the place to go into such things. Why I am here is of more immediate importance at this time.'

'Why you're here?' Caroline's fingers massaged the carved wood in her grasp. 'But why you're here has nothing to do with me.'

'You are wrong,' he retorted grimly. 'It has much to do with you. Unfortunately, that is why it must be kept—confidential.'

Caroline was more confused than ever. 'Why?'

Luis expelled his breath heavily. 'Tia Isabel sent for me. My brother is ill——'

'You mean—he's dying?' Caroline was appalled, but Luis quickly shook his head.

'No,' he said flatly, fingering the crucifix at his belt. 'I was not brought here to administer to him. He has merely developed a fever, as the result of exposure, and with bed rest he should recover completely.'

'Then what——'

'It is the state of his mind which concerns Tia Isabel,' declared Luis quietly. 'He has been—how do you say it?—making certain wild statements concerning your relationship.'

'O-our relationship?' Caroline's lips parted. 'I don't understand.'

Luis moistened his lips. 'He seems to be of the opinion that you—will change your mind.'

'No!'

'But yes. And Tia Isabel thought I should be informed.' His twisted smile was wry. 'Not because she has any liking for you, *señorita*, it must be said, but because she does not wish the name of Montejo to once again suffer the blight of another scandal.'

'An-another scandal?'

Luis bent his head. 'You told me Esteban had explained our relationship.'

'Well, yes.' Caroline licked her lips. 'You mean——'

Luis sighed. 'Esteban's mother killed herself. She was the victim of our father's intrinsic indifference to anyone's interests but his own.' He paused. 'My mother suffered some guilt, I know, but she was as helpless to resist his charm and attentions as anyone else.' He shrugged. 'He was that kind of man. He inspired affection in both men and women alike.

As you do! thought Caroline urgently; but she said nothing.

'So you see, Tia Isabel is concerned about what may happen when Esteban is well again. She wishes you should leave as soon as possible. And I endorse that view.'

Caroline's lips quivered. Of course. He would, she thought bitterly. So long as she was here at San Luis, she was both a threat and a temptation.

'I see,' she said now, looking down at the soft folds of apple-green satin that clothed her body so closely. 'So what have you decided?'

'You will leave tomorrow,' said Luis expressionlessly. 'Tomas will drive you to Las Estadas, and from there you can pick up the bus to Merida.' He shook his head. 'The arrangements are not entirely to my satisfaction, I will admit, but it is the way you came, and it is the best I can offer. Tomas will see you safely aboard the interstate transport, and once in Merida you should have no difficulty in booking a flight to London.'

'Thank you.'

Caroline tried to speak composedly, but the words were husky, and Luis noticed.

'You will be happier in England, as you say,' he intoned heavily 'With your own family and—friends.' He paused. 'Tell me, this man you had an affair with—you will meet with him again?'

His voice had harshened, and Caroline glanced at him a little apprehensively, suddenly aware of the lateness of the hour, and their unwilling isolation in this quiet room.

'Andrew?' she ventured carefully. 'Well, yes. I may see him. He—he and his wife live quite near us. He—he's a lecturer at the same university as—as my father.'

Luis's face was a graven mask. 'And he is the kind of man you most admire,' he continued, in the same tormented tone. 'A man of culture and sophistication, who treats you as his intellectual equal, and can sustain your interest?'

Caroline swallowed rather convulsively. 'He—he is an intelligent man, yes,' she admitted, and then: 'Luis, why are you telling me this? What does it matter to you how I intend to live my life? You don't want me——'

'Do not be a fool!' With a muttered curse Luis stretched out a hand, and in a swift sure movement grasped her arm and drew her closely against him. Through the rough wool of his gown, and the thin transparency of hers, the hard muscles of his body bit into her, the male scent of his skin invading every corner of her nasal passages. Her face was scraped by the coarse fibres of his robe, her lips parted, but suffocatingly deprived of air, her hands curling against him impotently, yet clutching the cloth where it came within her reach. 'Of a surety, I want you,' he grated, his mouth against the silky softness of her hair. 'And not even my mother, and the humiliations heaped upon her, can prevent me from admitting that I am as weak as my father was——'

Caroline's murmur of protest was stifled against his lips, breathed into his mouth, and melted by the heat of his passion. No gentleness this, but the eager hungry urgency that demanded complete surrender. One hand was gripping her nape, holding her still for his possession,

the other loosening the cord of her negligee, sliding beneath over the smooth sensuous down of the satin. Her
nightgown was low at the back, and his fingers found the
deep vee and caressed the sensitive curve of her spine. She
arched against him involuntarily, and a mindless sweetness invaded her senses. She had hardly known what it
was to want a man, to feel the need that tore away inside
her, like a living thing, fighting for survival. She wanted to
feel him close to her, without the restricting confines of
their clothes. Almost blindly, she pressed herself against
him, eager for whatever he cared to do with her.

'*Por Dios*, Luis!'

The choked exclamation came from the open doorway.
Doña Isabel stood in the aperture, a brocade robe concealing her nightgown, her dark hair two stubby plaits on
either side of her appalled face. That Luis turned at once
from Caroline in no way seemed to appease her. Her wild
eyes glittered with a malevolent fire, and Caroline, frantically drawing the folds of her negligee around her, knew
a moment's terror that the old lady might indeed have
lost her reason.

Luis went towards her, his shoulders expressing the
grim contrition that had twisted his face as he turned
away. Caroline, still at the mercy of her emotions, ad-
mired his repossession of control, even while she ached
with the awareness of its finality. Whatever happened,
they would never have another chance of being alone
together, Doña Isabel would see to that, and while she
knew she should despise herself for promoting his self-con-
tempt, she *couldn't*. Deep inside her, she knew that had
Doña Isabel not interrupted them, Luis would not have
been capable of denying her, and once they had been
lovers, surely he could not then have turned away? He
was not meant for a life of celibacy. Whatever promises
his mother had dragged from him, he was a man first, not
a priest, and her nails dug into her palms as his aunt

delivered her incomprehensible tirade.

'It is all right, *tia*,' Luis interrupted her at last, raising his hand in a gesture of defeat. He glanced bleakly towards Caroline, and she saw indeed that what she had feared had happened. 'I lost my head, that is all.' His mouth compressed, and he looked back at his aunt. 'Do not look so shocked, *tia*. It will never happen again.'

'The girl is leaving?' It was a statement, rather than a question, delivered in English, as her accusations had not been, and Luis inclined his head.

'Tomorrow,' he agreed flatly. 'You will arrange for Tomas to take her?'

Doña Isabel looked venomously at Caroline. 'I will arrange it,' she agreed, and turning stalked haughtily away.

'Luis——'

Almost as soon as his aunt had disappeared from her sight, Caroline whispered his name, taking a step towards him appealingly and putting out her hands in mute supplication, but Luis's face was stark and cold.

'Goodbye,' he said, and his voice was as chilling as his appearance. 'My aunt is right. You are a danger—to all of us!'

Caroline quivered. 'Is that what she said?'

'In essence,' he agreed heavily. '*Adios, señorita. Mucha suerte!*'

'*Luis!*'

She said his name again, but he had gone, and she was left speaking to an empty room. She said his name many times, after she had crawled into the opulent luxury of the bed, but nothing, and no one, could assuage her grief.

She packed her bags before breakfast, and by the time Carmencita brought her tray she had them safely stowed in the bathroom. The last thing she wanted was to draw attention to her departure, and knowing how the servants talked, she intended to behave just as if nothing unusual was about to happen.

She had not slept after Luis's departure, and her eyes felt sticky and her head ached, but she managed to drink two cups of coffee as a restorative, and was tense and apprehensive, when a knock came at her door.

It was Doña Isabel, as she was used to seeing her, bedecked in all her finery, jewels glittering on every finger, her headdress coiled above heavy gold earrings. If her eyes still glittered with the same malevolent light they had shown the night before, Caroline chose not to see them, inclining her head and listening politely to what the old lady had to say.

'You will conduct lessons with Emilia as usual this morning, *señorita*,' she announced bleakly, causing Caroline to look up in surprise. 'Well,' she continued, 'you do not wish for your departure to be made public, do you, *señorita*? Is it not simpler to leave this afternoon, while the—household is taking *siesta*?'

Caroline had to concede that the plan had some merit, after she had recovered from the immediate shock of knowing she was not leaving immediately. 'Will—will you say goodbye to Emilia for me, *señora*?' she ventured tautly. 'I—I regret—disappointing her like this. Please ask her to forgive me.'

'Emilia will soon forget you, *señorita*,' retorted Doña Isabel, without sympathy. 'Sooner or later my nephew will marry again, and when he does Emilia will learn to love her stepmother.'

'Yes, *señora*.'

Caroline spoke politely, but although she expected the old lady to leave her, Doña Isabel lingered a little longer.

'Why did you have to corrupt Luis?' she demanded suddenly, staring at the girl with those wild accusing eyes. 'He was a man, not like his brother, but you tried to destroy him!'

'That's not true!' Caroline's face was burning, but she managed to answer her. 'Luis—I—it was inevitable. I didn't cause it to happen. It just did.'

Doña Isabel snorted contemptuously. 'You expect me to believe that?'

'Yes.' Caroline sought for words to defend herself. 'Why—why, you yourself accused him of having a woman in the village!'

'*Quia!* What nonsense is this?'

'You did. You did!' Caroline linked and unlinked her fingers. 'That night—at dinner. The night you complained to Don Esteban about the woman using the—the *puerta accesoria*——'

'Pah! Stupid girl!' Doña Isabel's lips curled. 'Did you really believe I was accusing Luis?' She shook her head. 'No. No, do you hear me? I pretended, because that was what Esteban wanted me to believe. But I knew the woman came—not to see Luis, but to see him!'

'Ana Pascale?' whispered Caroline faintly, and Doña Isabel looked taken aback.

'That is her name!' she granted harshly. 'How do you know? Who told you? Not—Esteban?'

'No. Luis,' replied Caroline, hardly understanding any of this. 'Then who is she?'

'You do not know? Luis did not tell you that?'

'Luis? No.' Caroline shook her head. 'Please——'

'Ana Pascale is his mother's sister's daughter!' spat Doña Isabel venomously.

'His cousin?'

'And Esteban's mistress!' announced the old lady scornfully. 'To save her family from being ejected from the pitiful holding which is all Esteban allows them!'

Caroline shook her head. 'I—I can't believe it.'

'Why not? Did not Luis explain why he is obliged to remain at the seminary? Did he not tell you of his brother's threats concerning his mother and her family?'

'No!' But a faint light was dawning. 'You mean, Esteban owns—everything?'

But Doña Isabel was turning away, her face twisted, as if she suspected she had said too much. And yet, as Caroline allowed what she had said to filter into her consciousness, she was left with the certain knowledge that so far as she was concerned, Luis was as remote from her as ever.

Emilia must have thought she was rather grumpy that morning, answering only when she was spoken to, conducting the lessons without her usual good humour. It was as well that Juanita and Victor were still absent. She did not think she could have handled an argumentative group.

Esteban did not appear for lunch, but Emilia volunteered the information that the doctor had visited the *hacienda* again that morning. 'They say he still has a fever,' she remarked indifferently. 'Are you going to see him, *señorita*? To apologise for leaving him to walk all the way home?'

'No.' Caroline's answer was too abrupt, and she qualified it hastily. It would not do to rouse any suspicions now. 'Your father left me, Emilia. I was expected to walk home. It wasn't my fault that he overturned the carriage.'

'Or that you got a ride home with Gerardo and his friends,' remarked Emilia dryly. 'Oh, yes, I know about that. Benito told me. Benito is a good friend. He tells me everything.'

Caroline acknowledged this, and to her relief, Emilia's nursemaid appeared a few moments later to take Emilia for her rest. But as the little girl left her, she put out her hand and touched her cheek.

'Goodbye, Emilia,' she said, forcing a faint smile to her lips, and Emilia pulled a face.

'*Hasta la vista, señorita,*' she responded, and Caroline

nodded her head because she didn't trust herself to speak.

Her cases were brought down and stowed in the Range Rover, and then Doña Isabel accompanied her to the top of the flight of steps. Although it was fine at the moment, and humid, too, it had been raining, and a faint mist was rising from the ground. This was how she would remember it, thought Caroline tremulously, the warmth, and the colour, and the damp smells of the garden—and Luis's face, fatigued by the tensions of suppressed passion.

Tomas stowed her bags into the back of the Range Rover, then joined her inside, seating himself behind the wheel. He seemed narrow-eyed and jumpy, and Caroline wondered why, but as he spoke no English, she looked forward to a silent journey.

Gomez opened the gates as they drove through, raising his battered hat as they passed, and Caroline's throat tightened. She had come here with such high hopes. Now they had all been dashed, and she was leaving like a stranger in the night. Only it wasn't night, and she was no stranger; only a half-frightened girl, caught in a trap she had scarcely apprehended.

After the rain of the past days, the ground under the vehicle's wheels was waterlogged and heavy, and the journey down to the village was a hair-raising one. Even going downhill, the wheels skidded to the edge of the road, spinning uselessly over ditches, before regaining purchase on the slippery ground. Caroline clung helplessly to her seat, trying not to watch Tomas too closely, but she couldn't help seeing how the Mexican's sweating hands had difficulty in holding on to the wheel.

About a mile beyond the village Tomas suddenly changed his tactics, pulling the vehicle off the road into a belt of trees. Caroline thought at first he was stopping to recover his nerve, but to her surprise, he glanced at her and said: 'Perdón, señorita!' and then thrust open his door and climbed out. Within seconds he had disappeared, running as if for his life, through the trees that eventually emerged on to the road again.

Caroline was stunned, as much by Tomas's uncharacteristic attitude as by any immediate fear for herself. What was wrong with the man? Hadn't he the nerve to drive her to Las Estadas? Did he suspect that Esteban did not know of her departure, and was alarmed that he might be blamed?

Caroline shook her head. Surely Doña Isabel had explained. Surely he understood that he was simply following orders. If Esteban was angry, his censure would fall on his daughter and his aunt, and Caroline knew a pang of remorse when she thought of Emilia's reaction to her disappearance.

Still, her most immediate need was to get to Las Estadas, and although if she drove the Range Rover it was going to be difficult for Tomas to explain, if that was the only way, she would have to do it.

This thought had barely surfaced when she heard footsteps coming through the trees, and she expelled her breath in relief. Of course—why hadn't she thought of that? Tomas had stopped for the most natural reason in the world, and had she been more premature, and driven away without him, he would surely have been very angry.

A smile forming on her lips at her own foolishness, she turned, only to feel the smile freezing on her lips like a grimace. It was not Tomas who swung open the door of the Range Rover and climbed in beside her, but Esteban, and for several blank seconds she could neither move nor articulate.

'Ah, *señorita*!' As he lounged into the seat beside her, he was smiling beneficently. 'Did you think to leave without saying goodbye? Shame on you, Miss Leyton!'

CHAPTER ELEVEN

IT was with an effort that Caroline struggled to regain her composure. 'What—what are you doing here, *señor?*' she asked, trying to appear calm and unperturbed by his appearance. 'I thought Tomas was driving me to Las Estadas.' There was no point in pretending she had been going anywhere else, with her suitcases plainly visible in the back of the vehicle. 'I thought you were ill, *señor.*'

'A cold, nothing more.' Esteban dismissed his condition with a careless wave of his hand, but Caroline could see it had been a little more than that. Whether he was cured or not she could not be sure, but certainly something had left dark rings around his eyes, and robbed his sallow face of all colour. 'So now,' he continued, firing the ignition, 'let us get on. It would not do for you to miss your bus, would it?'

And have to spend another night at the inn, Caroline reflected uneasily, finishing what had been implicit in Esteban's statement, and she wondered how on earth he had learned she was leaving.

The Range Rover squelched out from the trees on to the road again, and Caroline half expected Esteban to turn back the way they had come. She couldn't believe he had arrived just to drive her to Las Estadas. It didn't make sense, and it was certainly out of character. But they turned away from San Luis, on the road that led through the semi-tropical terrain that lay between them and Las Estadas, and Caroline expelled her breath unevenly, wondering what, if anything, he intended to do with her. There were many miles between San Luis and Las Estadas, areas of jungle and vegetation, where a person could disappear and never be found again. Within weeks her bones would be picked dry by the predators that roamed the forest, and her whole body came out in a cold sweat at the thought of such a fate.

'You seem—dismayed, *señorita*,' Esteban remarked suddenly, breaking in on her morbid thoughts and causing her to look at him apprehensively. 'Why should the idea of myself driving you to Las Estadas worry you so much? We have driven this way before.'

Caroline's tongue circled her dry lips. 'Why didn't you drive me from the *hacienda*, then, *señor*? Why didn't you tell your aunt that you would take me to Las Estadas?'

'But I did.' Esteban sounded quite put out, and Caroline stared at him disbelievingly. 'It is true,' he persisted. 'It was I who suggested you leave after lunch. I am afraid I had an appointment with the doctor this morning, and therefore it was impossible for me to get away.'

Caroline could not comprehend what he was saying. 'Your—aunt—Doña Isabel *knew*?'

'But of course.' Esteban half smiled. 'Tia Isabel tells me everything. Did you not know?'

'No.' Caroline's response was barely audible. But at least she now knew how Esteban had found out she was leaving. Did he also know about Luis's visit the night before?

'I insisted on taking you myself,' Esteban added now. 'It was the least I could do after our last—confrontation. But I had business in the village, and I suggested Tomas should bring you on the first stage of the journey and meet me here.' He paused to allow another vehicle to pass them, a hazardous venture at the best of times, and doubly so now with the roads slippery and streaming with water. 'I wanted to apologise,' he went on. 'To ask you to forgive my selfish temper.'

Caroline would have thought his behaviour had had more serious overtones than a mere flash of temper, but his explanations were relieving her so much she was prepared to believe almost anything, just to get the journey over. Afterwards, she would consider why Tomas should have apologised to her as he got out of the vehicle, why he should have stopped in such a remote spot to change drivers, and why Doña Isabel, who had pretended to be helping her, should have reported all her doings to her nephew. But for now, she acknowledged his apology with a forced smile, and crossed her fingers tightly as the Range Rover turned a corner a little too fast and skidded to the edge of the track.

'So,' Esteban glanced her way, 'you are feeling better now, *señorita*? You do not think Esteban is such a villain, after all.'

Caroline shook her head. 'I—I never thought you were a villain, *señor*.'

'No?' He sounded sceptical. 'But you would rather believe my brother than me, no?'

Caroline caught her lower lip between her teeth. 'I beg your pardon?'

'Luis. You believe everything Luis has told you.'

'He has told me nothing, *señor*.'

'No?' Esteban blatantly did not believe her, and the feeling of unease rekindled inside her. 'He did not tell you that like Tia Isabel, my mother was a little—how shall I put it?—unusual?'

'No.' Caroline spoke firmly this time. 'Why should he tell me that? Your—your aunt is as sane as you or I.'

'Hmm.' Esteban absorbed this, while Caroline's pulse fluttered a little faster. 'Nevertheless, it has to be said that my mother was a little strange. Of course, Tia Isabel believes that my father was responsible for her condition. He was—fond of women, *señorita*. He had many mistresses.'

Caroline did not make any response. She hoped if she said nothing he would eventually grow tired of baiting her, but she should have known that Esteban enjoyed the pursuit as much as the capture.

'Of course,' he continued, 'after Mamá was dead, and he married Luis's mother, he became a model husband. I do not know what Irena had, but she kept him home at nights, and for that I should admire her.' He laughed at this, then broke off to cough rather hoarsely, as the legacy of the chill he had taken racked his lungs. 'Luis, of course, was the apple of her eye, but not of my father's, obviously. Else why did he leave the estate to me, and nothing to his wife's precious bastard!'

'Luis is not a bastard!' Caroline could keep silent no longer. 'He—he's just as much your father's son as you are. And—and it's unfair that the estate should not be divided.'

'Ah, yes.' Esteban glanced at her again, his eyes more speculative now, and Caroline wished he would keep his eyes on the road. It was too precarious a route to treat so contemptuously, and the adrenalin pumped through her veins as they careered across the road, narrowly missing an enormous pothole.

'I suppose Luis told you what happened to his mother after my father died?'

Caroline hesitated. 'He told me she entered a convent, yes.'

'Yes—a convent.' Esteban's lips curled. 'She knew I would not allow her to stay at San Luis, so she took the easy way out, eh?'

Caroline moved her shoulders helplessly. 'It's nothing to do with me, señor.'

Esteban shrugged. 'She thought she was so clever.'

'Clever, señor?' Caroline was confused.

'Yes, clever,' repeated Esteban harshly. 'She knew I hated her. And Luis. She knew that once Papa was dead I would do anything in my power to get rid of them.' He sneered. 'She thought that by entering the convent she had thwarted me.' He laughed again, but it was not a pleasant sound and Caroline shivered. 'She thought Luis would be more than a match for me. But she had forgotten about the rest of her family.'

'The rest of her family?' Caroline couldn't help the involuntary question, and he nodded.

'The Pascales. They live on the estate. They were my father's tenants. How else do you think he met Luis's mother?' His mouth twisted. 'Peasants, all of them! Unfit to mingle their blood with ours!'

Caroline was beginning to understand. Doña Isabel had spoken of the Pascales. Of Luis's cousin, Maria. But where did Luis come in?

'My father had Luis educated, of course,' Esteban continued now. 'For a peasant, he is remarkably intelligent.'

Caroline's nails dug painfully into her palms, but she kept silent, and he went on:

'My father sent him to the university of California. He gained a degree in agricultural studies. To help my father run the estate, you understand?'

Caroline nodded, not trusting herself to speak, and Esteban went on with his monologue.

'He came home with many—radical ideas. Ideas concerned with social conditions, and democratising the rights of the *peons*.' He shook his head. 'My father pretended to listen to him. He even agreed to try some of his methods. But fortunately a seizure robbed him of the power to speak or move and he was a living vegetable until his death.'

Caroline caught her breath. 'He was your father!'

'He was not fit to be my father at the end. He had destroyed everything my family ever stood for. He had mingled the blood of *conquistadores* with that of slaves, and he deserved to die!'

Caroline shook her head. 'And—and afterwards?' She had to know.

'Afterwards, as I said, Luis's mother entered the convent. She thought she had won. That Luis would stay here at the *hacienda*, and share the running of the estate. She knew he was stronger than I was, that he was not afraid of horses, as I was, and that the men would be loyal to him.' He smiled unpleasantly. 'But unfortunately she had forgotten Luis is also an honourable man. When I put it to him that his mother's family might fare badly if they were deprived of their small holding, he understood—particularly as he knew that being forced to leave their home would kill his aunt and uncle.'

Caroline's lips trembled. 'Why are you telling me all this, *señor*?'

'I thought you would like to know,' remarked Esteban airily. 'Just in case you had any foolish ideas that Luis might come after you.' He shook his head. 'Luis will not betray his family, *señorita*, and after all, why should he, for a harlot such as you!'

Caroline flinched as if he had struck her. And like a snake, she supposed he had. He had destroyed any hopes she might have nurtured that Luis might change his mind, and finally bestowed upon her an ugly epithet, such as he had previously reserved for Luis's mother. She had been right to feel afraid of him, to be apprehensive of the outcome of this journey. He had insulted her and abused her, and she felt as unclean as his words had made her.

'Have you nothing to say in your own defence, *señorita*?' he taunted now, and she saw to her relief that they were nearing the outskirts of Las Estadas. The journey was almost over, and she could hardly wait to be free of him.

'Well?' he persisted. 'Is it not true that you have a lover in England? A lover, moreover, who already has a wife?'

Caroline stiffened, and then realising Doña Isabel must have told him this too, she straightened her spine and answered him. 'I have no lovers, *señor*,' she declared coldly. 'Unlike your pitiful aunt and her sister, and Señorita Calveiro, I find more satisfaction in books and learning than prostrating myself before some ignorant *macho*!'

Esteban sucked in his breath. 'Have a care, *señorita*. You are not in England yet. And a woman like you should welcome any man's attentions!'

Caroline refused to look at him, even while the blood was pounding through her head, and apprehension overwhelmed her previous recklessness. Yet what could he do now? she argued with herself, as the shabby streets of Las Estadas engulfed them—but she could find no comfort in the fateful question.

The bus station, she knew, was at the far side of the town, a corrugated-roofed building, with a small office for booking tickets. The bus services in Mexico were surprisingly good, and although it had been a tiring journey, Caroline had not found the trip from Merida to Las Estadas uncomfortable. Now, however, she didn't much care whether the coming trip was comfortable or not. She just wanted to escape from Esteban's company, and the cruel crudity of his tongue.

Esteban did not take the main road through the town. He turned left into a narrower street, lined with closely-packed houses, and smelling of stale food and unwashed humanity. Caroline was not immediately dismayed. She thought it might be a more direct route to the bus station. She had still to ascertain that there was transport out of Las Estadas this evening, but surely Doña Isabel would not have let her come without being sure. And then she remembered, Doña Isabel was not to be trusted, and Luis had expected her to leave that morning.

Fear feathered over her skin like a cobweb's touch. The truth was, she was putting her faith in a man who had professed to despise her. She already knew what he was like. She had no need to doubt the flaws in his character. And remembering the butterfly, she wondered if she had any more chance of escaping unscathed.

When Esteban brought the Range Rover to a halt beside a pair of ramshackle wooden gates, her heart almost stopped beating. This was definitely not the bus station, and she glanced at him anxiously, trying to hide her fear.

'Where are we?' she asked, trying to remain cool. 'What is this place? Why have we stopped here?'

Esteban smiled, but the mobility of his mouth did not reach his eyes. They were still as hard and calculating as ever, and Caroline felt the sweat break out on her palms. 'One moment, *señorita*,' he told her lightly, pushing open his door and climbing down from the cab. 'I have some small business to attend to. I will join you shortly!' and slamming the door behind him, he sauntered through the sagging gates.

Caroline could hardly stop her knees from shaking. Specks of rain splattered the windscreen, and the sky had grown darker, casting gloomy shadows down the main street. Where were they? she wondered, too conscious of her own vulnerability to try and investigate. If only she understood the language, she thought desperately. But it was too late now to wish something like that.

Another van stopped behind them, and glancing round, she saw two men unloading some crates. Their contents appeared to be bottles of some sort, and she watched them half idly, still absorbed with her own problems. It was only when they pushed the wooden gates wide and she could see the back of the building that comprehension dawned. It was the inn, she could swear it. The man were carrying in crates of beer and *tequila*. And as if to confirm this, Esteban emerged from the building at that moment, accompanied by Señor Allende. He was gesturing towards the Range Rover as he spoke, evidently unaware that she could see them, but judging by the malicious amusement that his words were engendering, her own predicament was being discussed.

Panic flared inside her. If Esteban was speaking to the innkeeper, a man whom previously he had despised, he had to have an ulterior motive. And she did not need a crystal ball to guess what he intended.

Battening down the hysteria that threatened to overwhelm her, she acted purely on instinct. Esteban had left the keys in the ignition, obviously never expecting her to touch them, but now she levered herself across the central console into the driving seat, and turned the ignition.

Esteban saw her as the engine fired, but although he broke into a run, with the fat little proprietor at his heels, they were much too late to stop her. Releasing the clutch at the same time as she pressed down hard on the accelerator, the vehicle practically leapt forward, and a giggle of hysteria escaped her as she careered wildly down the street.

She had no idea which way the bus station lay. She drove purely on instinct as she had done everything else, but fate, or the gods, call it what you will, must have been on her side, for as she emerged into the main street again she saw the roof of the bus station only a few yards ahead of her.

She guessed Esteban would follow her, but she had to risk it. Somehow, it didn't matter how, she was taking a bus out of Las Estadas tonight, and she didn't much care where it took her.

An hour later, seated on the bus to Merida, she reviewed the events leading up to her departure with a sense of incredulity. As she had expected, Esteban had come after her, but for once the fact that she was English proved a blessing. Waiting at the bus station, for the very bus she wanted to board, was a party of British tourists, who had been spending three days visiting archaeological sites in the area, and hearing their familiar voices, she had quickly introduced herself. Her explanation that she had taken a job in the area which hadn't worked out evoked some raised eyebrows among the older ladies of the group, but her smile, which felt glued to her face, was so appealing they were forced to believe her.

Esteban arrived, hot and irate, as they were boarding the streamlined vehicle which was to take them to Merida. Señor Allende was still with him, panting to keep up with Esteban's longer stride, and Caroline suspected it was to him she owed her freedom. Alone, Esteban might have inspired some credibility, but with the fat, perspiring little proprietor beside him, he assumed an air of seedy respectability, which was not at all convincing. His story that Caroline was leaving his employ without gaining permission or giving notice was received with tight-lipped disapproval, and it was soon obvious that the ladies of the party thought Caroline had had a lucky escape. Esteban's imperious attitude did not impress them, and they grew quite indignant on her behalf when he threatened her with legal action.

'I suggest you take it up with the Consulate,' suggested one elderly female, viewing the innkeeper's sweat-streaked face with distaste. 'I'm sure they'll be quite willing to help you, if you feel some compensation is necessary.'

'Oh, yes,' Esteban's mouth twisted as he watched Caroline climb aboard the bus, 'I shall have compensation, *señora*. You can be assured of that!' and as he strode away, Caroline realised that someone else would pay for this afternoon's work.

She hoped it would not be Emilia. As she remembered the child as she had last seen her, her heart ached abominably. But what could she do? she asked herself despairingly. Esteban held all the cards, and she could only blame his father for the unjust terms of his will. If he had cared for Luis's mother, as he must have done to marry her and remain faithful to her, why had he not kept faith with their child? Esteban and Luis should have shared the estate, and any honourable man would have known that. But Esteban was not an honourable man; he was coarse and insensitive, vindictive to the point of cruelty, and incapable of inspiring anything but bitterness and fear in the people who served him.

CHAPTER TWELVE

THERE was an autumn chill in the air as Caroline walked home from the station. Already the summer was over, and the previous night's wind had brought a showering of gold and amber leaves to cover the grass. It would be October soon, the start of the university year, but for her there were no new beginnings.

She had managed to find a job in a travel agent's. It was not really the kind of occupation she wanted, but all the teaching vacancies had been filled by now, and besides, she had not yet decided that that was what she wanted to do either.

Somehow, since her return from Mexico four weeks ago, she had found it almost impossible to settle to anything. What had once absorbed her now seemed only faintly interesting, and the idea of going on and furthering her career had lost its initial spark. How amused Esteban would be, if he knew, she thought bitterly, unable to dispel the images that persistently tormented her mind. She, the quintessential career girl, would have given everything she possessed to be one man's wife . . .

Luis! She thrust her hands more deeply into the pockets of her creamy leather jacket, feeling the familiar weakness the thought of him evoked. She wondered if he ever thought of her in his lonely monastic cell, or whether time and separation had achieved for him what it could not achieve for her. Perhaps his religion was enough. Perhaps it was sufficient compensation. But for her, there was only pain and emptiness, and the certain knowledge that this time there was no escape.

Seeing Andrew again had not helped. She had wondered whether, meeting him again, she would feel any of the old excitement his presence used to generate, but it hadn't worked. He was like an old friend, nothing more, and she was glad she had never permitted their relationship to extend beyond the bounds of a tender flirtation. She liked him. She supposed she always would. And certainly she sympathised with the difficulties he experienced in his marriage. But her own feelings for him had fallen into perspective, and what she had imagined was love had been merely hero-worship.

Now she crossed the square and turned into the quiet mews where her parents' house was situated. It was early evening, and already the shadows were casting pools of darkness between the burgeoning illumination of the street lamps. Soon it would be dark before she left the office, and the real winter nights would begin, nights when she would have more than enough time to fear the future and regret the past.

There were lights already in her parents' house, flooding out over the neatly-painted windowboxes that her mother tended with such care. The cobbled court before the house was occupied by her father's shabby Rover, that he refused to part exchange despite her mother's urgings, and the doors to the garage had been opened to reveal her mother's smarter Mini. That her father hadn't immediately put the Rover into the garage was a source of wonder to her, and she guessed something must have happened to interrupt his usual routine.

Without feeling any real sense of apprehension, she inserted her key in the lock and entered the house as usual, calling out a greeting to her mother as she hung her coat in the hall. So far as she was concerned, she was glad to be home, and the warm sense of security it gave her wrapped itself around her like a second skin. Her parents had never interfered in her life, and they had accepted her explanation that the job in Mexico hadn't worked out with only a degree of speculation. But now, when her mother emerged into the hall to confront her, there was a definite look of anticipation on her face, and Caroline felt her own colour falter when Mrs Leyton hastily closed the sitting room door behind her.

'You have a visitor,' she said at once, in an undertone. 'Two visitors, in fact. Señor de Montejo, and—and Emilia!'

Caroline groped weakly for the banister. 'Did—did you say—Señor de Montejo?'

'That's right.' Her mother wrung her hands anxiously. 'You'd better come in. Your father's just offered him a drink, but I think you ought to come and speak to him.' She paused. 'He—well, he wants you to go back and take up your teaching job again, and when I told him you were not likely to agree, he said he hoped he'd be able to make you change your mind.'

Caroline was trembling. She had never expected this to happen. When she had left Esteban at the bus station she had known he was angry, but she had never dreamed he would follow her to London, or involve her parents in his sordid affairs.

'I—I don't want to see him,' she said now, glancing about her anxiously. 'Oh, Mum, I really don't want to see him.'

'Why not?' Her mother looked at her reprovingly. 'Caroline, I really think you ought. He's travelled all this way. Don't you think it's the least you can do?'

'No——'

'Caroline, be reasonable!'

'I am being reasonable.' Caroline could feel the panic rising inside her. 'I—I—it's four weeks since I left Mexico. If—if he was so keen to retain my services, he should have contacted me before I got another job.'

'Well, apparently his brother died——' began Mrs Leyton thoughtfully, marshalling her argument, then exclaimed: 'Caroline! Oh, dear heaven!' as her daughter slumped in a dead faint at the foot of the stairs.

'Do you think I should call the doctor?'

Caroline came round to the sound of her mother's voice speaking softly somewhere nearby, but when her eyes opened it was not either of her parents who was gazing down at her.

'*Luis?*' she breathed, convinced she must be dreaming, and then more strongly: 'Luis, what are you doing here?' as he came down on the side of the couch on which she was lying.

'*Salud, pequeña,*' he murmured softly, laying one of his hands over both of hers where they were pressed together at her midriff. 'I did not realise my arrival would be so traumatic for you.' He paused, his grey eyes dark with emotion. 'Would you prefer we should leave and come back later?'

'No——'

Caroline's involuntary denial, and her feeble attempt to struggle up from the pillows, attracted her parents' attention. They had been talking quietly together, near the sitting room door, but now they turned and gazed anxiously at her, and at the man towards whom she was gazing so eagerly.

But it was someone else who interrupted them, someone small and dark and excited, dressed more suitably than Caroline had ever seen her, in a pretty fringed suede skirt and jacket, and a simple woollen jumper.

'Señorita, señorita!' she exclaimed, jumping up from the chair on which she had been sitting, as soon as she saw Caroline was conscious. 'Señorita, we have come to take you back to San Luis with us. Say you will come, please, say you will come! Tio Vincente so much wants you to live with us.'

Caroline could only shake her head, staring at Emilia as if she couldn't believe her eyes, and this time Luis intervened, drawing Emilia to his side with a gentle insistence, raising his finger warningly as she started to protest.

'It is too soon,' he assured her quietly, as Caroline glanced round at her mother and father, wondering how they were taking all this. 'Miss Leyton got quite a shock to find us here. I think we should go away now, and leave her to recover.'

'No!' Caroline's voice was firmer, as she clutched at Luis's hand. 'No, please——' She cast another imploring glance at her parents. 'I mean, I have got over it. I am all right, honestly.' She struggled into a sitting position, gazing at him wonderingly. 'Luis, please—tell me why you're here.'

'You know that already,' put in Mrs Leyton dryly, crossing the floor to the couch and looking down at her daughter with half impatient eyes. 'Caroline, I told you what Señor de Montejo had said, but you refused to see him. Do I take it now that you've changed your mind?'

'She was shocked, Elizabeth.' Caroline's father joined the group around the couch. 'How are you feeling, darling? I've never known you pass out like that before.'

'I'm fine, Daddy.' Caroline was clinging to Luis's hand as if she would never let him go, and her parents exchanged helpless glances. 'I—I didn't know you meant—Luis, you see.'

'I think we've gathered that, Caroline,' her mother responded dryly. 'I suppose it was my fault. I should have explained. But how was I to know you were likely to react so violently?'

Caroline shook her head, looking at Luis urgently. 'She—she said you—your brother is dead. Is that true?' She caught her lower lip between her teeth as she met Emilia's dark eyes. 'I—I can hardly believe it.'

'There was a car crash.' It was Emilia who spoke. 'On the way back from Las Estadas. Señor Allende was driving, but the roads were slippery——'

'What?' Caroline gasped, and her returning colour receded again. 'Luis—do you mean——'

'I think we ought to leave them alone, Elizabeth.' Mr Leyton could sense the tenseness of the atmosphere, and Caroline's mother pulled herself together and nodded in agreement.

'Yes. Yes. I—I'll make some tea,' she said, and then, glancing at Emilia, she said: 'Would you like to come and help me, young lady? I think your uncle would prefer to speak with—with Caroline alone.'

Emilia looked doubtful, but Luis finally extracted his hand from Caroline's and rose firmly to his feet. 'I think that is a very good idea, Emilia,' he averred, propelling her gently away from him. 'Miss Leyton and I do have some private matters to discuss. Perhaps Mrs Leyton will let you pour out the milk for her, while her daughter and I discuss the possibilities of her returning to Mexico with us, hmm?'

'You won't go away?'

Obviously, for all her apparent indifference to her father's death, Emilia was still very much a child, and as a child she craved security, and Luis shook his head.

'I promise I shall be here, all the time,' he assured her softly. 'Thank you.' This to Caroline's mother. 'I am most grateful.'

Caroline's mother made a deprecating gesture, then ushered Emilia ahead of her out of the room. Mr Leyton closed the door behind them, and the silence that followed their departure was broken only by Caroline's unsteady breathing.

'Esteban is dead,' she whispered, still hardly able to believe it. 'Because—because of me——'

'*Porqueria*, of course not.' Luis turned to face her tautly. 'Tomas was to take you to Las Estadas, and I hazard a guess that Tomas would not have turned the car off the road. Esteban was drunk, and so was Allende, so far as we can gather. He must have been, to have attempted the journey in that condition.'

Caroline shook her head. 'It doesn't seem possible.'

'Why?' Luis paced restlessly across the hearth and back again. 'Because of what he threatened you with? Because you were afraid it was he, and not I, who had come to find you?'

Caroline swung her legs to the floor, pushing back her hair with an unsteady hand. 'How—how do you know about that?'

'How do you think?' Luis made a sound of impatience. 'Where do you think they did their drinking? At the hotel, of course. There are a dozen witnesses there willing to say that Esteban threatened you with beating, raping, and worse!' His dark face was grim. 'God knows what he might have done had he reached San Luis alive. One thing is certain: Emilia and Tia Isabel would have borne the brunt of his fury.'

Caroline's tongue circled her lips as she looked up at him. 'How—how did you find out?'

'About what? The fact that your departure had been delayed—or Esteban's accident?'

Caroline frowned. 'Well—the accident, I suppose.'

'I arrived on the scene only minutes after it had happened,' Luis retorted curtly, and as she gazed at him incredulously, he went on: 'It was Emilia who told me what had happened.'

'Emilia?'

'Yes,' Luis nodded. 'You see, you had not told her you were leaving, but when, that afternoon, she visited her friend Benito, he confided what had happened.'

'A—about Esteban?'

'But of course. By then Tomas had come back, and the servants knew what was going on. It was a source of excitement to them, that the *patrón* should get up from his sick bed to follow the young English lady to Las Estadas.'

'But—Emilia——'

Luis sighed, spreading his hands. 'She thought he had dismissed you. You know how her imagination works. She was afraid, but for different reasons.'

'And she sent for you?'

'Tomas—reluctantly agreed to call at the seminary.'

Caroline shook her head. 'And?'

Luis made a sound of self-derision. '*Dios mio*, you can have no idea how I felt when I heard what had happened.'

Caroline got rather falteringly to her feet. 'He—he might have had the best of intentions.'

Luis bent his head. 'He might. But I had to be sure.' He thrust his hands behind his back, and she could see the tautness of his muscles beneath the fine cloth. 'I was afraid—I was afraid that he——'

'—might touch me?' she ventured softly, and he nodded. 'Did he?'

'No.' She shook her head again, and quickly explained what had happened. 'I don't know what I'd have done without the others,' she admitted, mentioning the tourist party she had joined. 'They—they were very kind to me. I—I flew back to London with them.'

'Thank God for that!' Luis's thanks were heartfelt.

Caroline managed a faint smile. 'When—when my mother—told me he—he was dead, I thought—I thought at first——'

'—she meant me?' Luis finished for her, and she inclined her head.

'That's why I fainted, I suppose. All—all the blood just seemed to drain out of me.'

'Oh, Caroline!'

With a groan of impatience he filled the space between them, stepping so close to her she almost lost her balance and collapsed on to the couch again.

'It is too soon, is it not?' he breathed, the lapels of his dark jacket brushing the swollen fullness of her breasts. 'I should not have come here yet. I should have written to you and told you what had happened, begged you in letter form to reconsider your decision.'

'My decision?' Caroline's voice had a tremor, but she didn't try to hide it. 'What decision?'

'The decision to come back to us,' exclaimed Luis huskily. 'We need you—Emilia needs you——'

'And—and you?' Caroline looked up at him, lifting her hands to finger the smooth satiny hide of his leather jacket. 'Do you need me, Luis?' She paused, then added recklessly: 'Because—because I need you——'

Her words were cut off by the probing pressure of his mouth. As if whatever will-power he had possessed had suddenly snapped, his arms were around her, hauling her closely against him, making her unmistakably aware that needing was not something peculiar to her. She could feel every stirring muscle of his body, and the searching possession of his kiss robbed her of what little strength remained in her legs. She sagged against him, shaking with reaction, and he bent to swing her up into his arms, looking down at her with eyes burning with passion.

'I need you,' he agreed thickly, as she looped her arms around his neck. 'And God knows, I've never said that to any woman before.'

Caroline pressed her face against his neck. 'But—the seminary——'

'I think you know now why I entered the seminary,' he said heavily, lounging into an armchair, with her on his lap. 'Tia Isabel told you, did she not?'

'And Esteban,' said Caroline softly, burrowing against him, parting the lapels of his jacket, and nestling against the soft silk of his shirt. 'In case I—I imagined you might—come after me.'

'Oh, *mi querida*, there was always that possibility.' He shook his head. 'Each time I saw you it was harder to go back—to go on with the life I had made for myself.' He bent his head to nuzzle his lips against her ear. 'And when Tomas brought the message that Esteban had taken you to Las Estadas——' He broke off with a sound of anguish. 'I knew that whatever happened, my immortal soul was not worth the sacrifice I was making.'

'Luis!' She cupped his face between her hands, gazing at him disbelievingly. 'You mean—you're not going back? Ever?'

'Did you doubt it?'

'I don't know. I was afraid to ask.' Caroline was so overwhelmed, she could hardly speak. 'Oh, Luis, I love you so much!'

'*Amada!*' His tongue probed the hollows of her ear, while his hand slid up to cradle her throat. 'Can you not feel I am trembling, *querida*? Believe me, I did not come here secure in your love. I was afraid—so afraid—that this man, this man you cared for might have replaced me completely in your affections.'

'Andrew?' Caroline lifted her face to his like a flower seeking the sun. 'Oh, Luis, I never loved Andrew. I realised that almost as soon as we met. He—I cared for him, I suppose, but not—not in the way I care for you.'

'*Dios gracias*,' muttered Luis fervently, before seeking her mouth with his once again.

Their kisses were becoming deeper, more passionate, and as if aware that her parents might intrude upon them at any time, Luis finally dragged himself away, to rest his head back against the soft upholstery.

'So,' he said, his eyes still drugged and sensual, 'you will come back with me?'

'If you want me to,' she agreed, loosening his tie and the top two buttons of his shirt, and bestowing a kiss on the brown column of his throat she had exposed. 'Hmm, your skin is slightly damp and salty——'

'—and over-stimulated,' he groaned hoarsely, pushing her teasing fingers away. 'Caroline, do not push me too far, I beg of you. I would not wish to embarrass your parents.'

'How would you do that?' she persisted, carrying his hand to her lips and allowing her tongue to probe his palm, so that with a smothered oath he bent his head, and substituted his mouth instead of his hand.

Her hands slid around his neck, tangling in the thick dark hair that grew down his nape, and she moaned in submission when his hand slid possessively over her thigh, and probed the inner curve of her leg.

'*Te deseo,*' he murmured urgently. 'I want you, *querida.* But not here, not like this. Even though you drive me to the edge of distraction!'

Caroline drew back to look at him. 'Do you love me?'

'Love you?' He gazed at her half ruefully. 'Oh, *pequeña,* loving is such a simple word to describe the way I feel. I adore you, I worship you! And yes, I love you, too, much more than you could ever imagine.'

Caroline thought about her next words before saying them: 'What—what about—Doña Isabel?'

'What about her?' Luis expelled his breath heavily, trying without too much success to control his emotions. 'Oh—you mean, because she told Esteban what you planned to do?'

'You know about that?'

'But of course. Tia Isabel and I have had some time to talk about the future.'

'A-and?'

'She knows of my feelings for you.' He sighed. 'It was this, as much as anything, which tipped the balance against you, I am afraid.'

Caroline shook her head. 'But why?'

Luis stroked her cheek. 'The night she sent for me, she was concerned about you, about what Esteban might do to you.' He shrugged. 'But then later, when she saw us together, her mind became confused, and the memories of what happened to Esteban's mother, her sister, became inextricably entangled with what she had seen. In her mind, you were a corrupting influence, and she turned to Esteban because he was there.'

Caroline shivered. 'She frightened me.'

'Do not be alarmed. She is no longer at San Luis. She left a few days after Esteban was buried. She has gone to stay with a friend of Señora Calveiro's, and afterwards she plans to return to Spain.'

'To Spain?' Caroline was amazed.

'I, too, was surprised,' Luis admitted. 'But you must remember, Isabel is no relation of mine. She was Esteban's aunt. My addressing her as *tia* was simply a courtesy title. Now that he is dead, she no longer has ties with the *hacienda*.'

Caroline tried to absorb this. 'So—so there'll be only— the three of us?'

'To begin with,' agreed Luis dryly, and her cheeks darkened with becoming colour. 'So long as you do not object to Emilia's presence.'

'Object?' Caroline gasped. 'How could I object? She has been through so much!'

Luis hesitated. 'You mean—Esteban's death?'

'Her father's death, yes.'

'Esteban was not her father,' Luis told her heavily, and Caroline felt a sudden chill.

'But—but you said—you told me——'

'I told you *I* was not her father,' Luis reminded her quietly. 'I did not say Esteban was.'

'Then—then who——'

Luis bent his head. 'He was a friend of mine, I regret,'

he conceded quietly. 'A visitor to the *hacienda*, at a time when Juana was most unhappy.'

'And Esteban knew this?'

'No.' Luis sighed. 'I think he secretly believed Emilia was his daughter, even though he allowed the fiction that she was mine to go unchallenged.'

'But—Emilia——'

'—knows the truth. Or at least, as much of it as it is necessary for her to know at this time.'

Caroline sighed. 'She so much wanted to be your daughter.'

Luis shrugged. 'And so she shall be. If you will let her live with us. And when there are other children,' he caressed her eyelids with his lips, 'she will be their older sister, hmm?'

'Whatever you say,' whispered Caroline softly, and he was bending to kiss her again when the door was peremptorily opened and the subject of their last discussion danced into the room.

'Tio Vincente! *Señorita*—oh!' This as Caroline scrambled up rather inelegantly from Luis's knee. Then, her lips quivering a little as she sought to be grown-up about it: 'You are going to marry Tio Vincente, after all!'

'If he'll have me,' Caroline agreed huskily, and bent to hug the little girl close to her as Luis accepted.

Three months later, Caroline returned home from Mariposa one morning to find her husband at work in his study as usual. Since Esteban's death much of the work that had previously fallen to the estate agent's shoulders was now shared by the master of the estate, and the desk which Caroline had previously found so empty and denuded of any correspondence was now much in use and littered with files and papers.

'Well?' asked Luis, getting to his feet as she came into the room, and coming round to put his hands on her shoulders.

'What did old Rivera say? Tell me at once. Is it what you suspected? *Nombre de Dios!* Do not keep me in suspense. I have done no work this morning. I wait only for your return. You should have let me come with you.'

'To hear that you're going to become a father in the near future?' remarked Caroline teasingly, looking up at him, and Luis's grey eyes narrowed.

'Then it is true?'

'It seems like it,' Caroline nodded.

'*Dios!*' Luis gazed down at her half impatiently. 'I knew I should have taken more care.'

'Why?' Caroline challenged him quietly. 'I didn't want you to.' She touched his belt insinuatively. 'I want your baby, Luis. I want us to have lots of babies.'

Luis's lean hands stilled her probing fingers. 'Caroline, be serious!' he exclaimed, even though his breathing had quickened in concert with hers. 'We have not even had a honeymoon yet!'

'We can have one afterwards,' said Caroline casually. 'You know Mummy and Daddy said they would like to come out here to visit. They can come after the baby is born, and we'll go away together, just the two of us.' She sighed ecstatically. 'Oh, Emilia's going to be so excited!'

'Caroline, are you sure you're all right!'

'Of course I'm all right.' Caroline pressed herself against him. 'Hmm, darling, you look tired. You're working too hard.'

'And getting too little sleep,' he agreed dryly, and her cheeks dimpled.

'Do you mind?' she murmured, and his eyes darkened with emotion.

'Caroline——'

'Love me,' she breathed against his mouth, and with a groan, Luis gave in to the temptation of her softly parted lips.

Some time later, in the twilit luxury of their bedroom, Luis levered himself up on one elbow to look down at the lissom beauty of his wife beside him. Feeling his eyes upon her, Caroline stirred sensuously, in no way embarrassed by his scrutiny. She was completely uninhibited in his presence, he had taught her to be that way, and she loved these moments in the aftermath of lovemaking, when he was so completely hers.

'I had some news myself this morning,' he murmured, as she lifted her hand to stroke a caressing finger down his chest. 'That rogue Vaquera rang me.'

'Vaquera?' Caroline frowned. 'Isn't he your solicitor or something?'

'He was my father's lawyer, and subsequently Esteban's,' Luis agreed, bending to touch her shoulder with his lips. 'As far as being mine is concerned, perhaps now he would like to be so.'

'Why? What do you mean?' Caroline moved her shoulder against his mouth with sinuous pleasure. 'What did he tell you?'

'Only that he had come across my father's last will and testament,' Luis informed her dryly, and smiled at her sudden arousal.

'Your father's last will and testament!' she echoed. 'You mean—there was a will involving you?'

'Apparently.' Luis subsided on to the pillows beside her again, putting a possessive hand on her still flat stomach. 'He says it must have been drawn up by one of the junior partners who has since left his employ, but my own opinion is that Esteban has been paying him to keep quiet.'

Caroline jack-knifed into a sitting position, one leg drawn up to support her chin. 'You mean—Esteban was bribing him to keep the will to himself?'

'Something like that,' agreed Luis with a shrug. Then: 'Come here! It's nothing to get so steamed up about.'

'It is so!' Caroline was indignant. 'Do you realise what this means?'

'It means that I now legally own, from my father,

something I previously owned on my brother's death,' observed Luis quietly. His eyes darkened sensually. 'Now, will you come here? Or shall I come to you?'

Caroline gazed at him in frustration. 'Luis, it means Esteban was depriving you of something that was rightfully yours,' she protested.

'But Esteban is dead,' remarked Luis flatly. 'And I have so much. How can I blame him now?'

Caroline sighed, but as his lazy fingers slid over her thigh from knee to hipbone, her protestations vanished beneath a tide of desire too strong to resist.

'But what about your mother?' she whispered finally, as his mouth sought the parted sweetness of hers. 'Will you tell her?'

'I will tell her,' agreed Luis, half impatiently, silencing her further with a breath-stopping kiss. 'But it will not make any difference to her. She is happy where she is. You know it. In that, as in all other things, Esteban was the loser.'

'You're very generous,' she breathed huskily, and his smile was triumphant.

'I can afford to be,' he assured her softly, and sought possession of that which was undeniably his.